"What do you want from me?" Lauren asked, her voice barely above a whisper.

And she thought that whatever happened, she would always remember the way Dominik smiled at her then, half wolf and all man. That it was tattooed inside her, branded into her flesh, forever a part of her. Whether she liked it or not.

"What I want from you, little red, is a wedding night."

Lauren's throat was almost too dry to work. She wasn't sure it would. "You mean...?"

"I mean in the traditional sense, yes. With all that entails."

He shifted, and she had never felt smaller. In the sense of being delicate. *Precious*, something in her whispered, though she knew that was fanciful. And, worse, foolish.

"Find a threshold, and I will carry you over it," he told her, his voice low and intent. And the look in his gray eyes was so male, very nearly *possessive*, it made her ache. "I will lay you down on a bed and I will kiss you awhile, to see where it goes. And all I need from you is a promise that you will not tell me what you do and do not like until you try it. That's all, Lauren. What do you have to lose?"

Conveniently Wed!

Conveniently wedded, passionately bedded!

Whether there's a debt to be paid, a will to be obeyed or a business to be saved...she's got no choice but to say, "I do!"

But these billionaire bridegrooms have got another think coming if they imagine marriage will be that easy...

Soon their convenient brides become the objects of inconvenient desire!

Find out what happens after the vows in:

Claiming His Christmas Wife by Dani Collins

My Bought Virgin Wife by Caitlin Crews

The Sicilian's Bought Cinderella by Michelle Smart

Crown Prince's Bought Bride by Maya Blake

Chosen as the Sheikh's Royal Bride by Jennie Lucas

Penniless Virgin to Sicilian's Bride by Melanie Milburne

Look for more Conveniently Wed! coming soon!

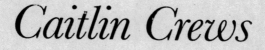

Caitlin Crews

UNTAMED BILLIONAIRE'S
INNOCENT BRIDE

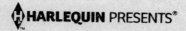

HARLEQUIN PRESENTS®

Recycling programs
for this product may
not exist in your area.

ISBN-13: 978-1-335-53840-6

Untamed Billionaire's Innocent Bride

First North American publication 2019

Copyright © 2019 by Caitlin Crews

Printed in U.S.A.

USA TODAY bestselling and RITA® Award–nominated author **Caitlin Crews** loves writing romance. She teaches her favorite romance novels in creative-writing classes at places like UCLA Extension's prestigious Writers' Program, where she finally gets to utilize the MA and PhD in English literature she received from the University of York in England. She currently lives in the Pacific Northwest with her very own hero and too many pets. Visit her at caitlincrews.com.

Books by Caitlin Crews

Harlequin Presents

Undone by the Billionaire Duke

Conveniently Wed!

Imprisoned by the Greek's Ring
My Bought Virgin Wife

One Night With Consequences

A Baby to Bind His Bride

Bound to the Desert King

Sheikh's Secret Love-Child

Stolen Brides

The Bride's Baby of Shame

The Combe Family Scandals

The Italian's Twin Consequences
Untamed Billionaire's Innocent Bride

Visit the Author Profile page
at Harlequin.com for more titles.

I can't believe that this is my 50th book for Harlequin! What a delightful ride it's been so far!

I want to thank Jane Porter, whose novels inspired me to try to write my first Presents and whose friendship, mentorship and stalwart sisterhood have changed my life in a million glorious ways.

I want to thank my two marvelous editors, Megan Haslam and Flo Nicoll, who I simply couldn't do without. What would these stories be without your guidance, encouragement, excitement, fantastic editing and endless help? I shudder to think! And I want to thank the wonderful Jo Grant as well, for always being such a shining light for category romance and those of us who write it.

But most of all I want to thank you, my readers, for letting me tell you my stories. Here's to fifty more!

xoxox

CHAPTER ONE

Lauren Isadora Clarke was a Londoner, born and bred.

She did not care for the bucolic British countryside, all that monotonous green with hedges this way and that, making it impossible to *get* anywhere. She preferred the city, with all its transportation options endlessly available—and if all else failed, the ability to walk briskly from one point to the next. Lauren prized punctuality. And she could do without stiff, uncomfortable footwear with soles outfitted to look like tire tread.

She was not a hiker or a rambler or whatever those alarmingly red-cheeked, jolly hockey-sticks sorts called themselves as they brayed about in fleece and clunky, sensible shoes. She found nothing at all entertaining in huffing up inclines only to slide right back down them, usually covered in the mud that accompanied all the rain that made

England's greenest hills that color in the first place. Miles and miles of tramping about for the dubious pleasure of "taking in air" did not appeal to her and never had.

Lauren liked concrete, bricks, the glorious Tube and abundant takeaways on every corner, thank you. The very notion of *the deep, dark woods* made her break out in hives.

Yet, here she was, marching along what the local innkeeper had optimistically called a road—it was little better than a footpath, if that—in the middle of the resolutely thick forests of Hungary.

Hive-free thus far, should she wish to count her blessings.

But Lauren was rather more focused on her grievances today.

First and foremost, her shoes were not now and never had been sensible. Lauren did not believe in the cult of *sensible shoes*. Her life was eminently sensible. She kept her finances in order, paid her bills on time, if not early, and dedicated herself to performing her duties as personal assistant to the very wealthy and powerful president and CEO of Combe Industries at a level of consistent excellence she liked to think made her indispensable.

Her shoes were impractical, fanciful creations that reminded her that she was a woman—which came in handy on the days her boss treated her as rather more of an uppity appliance. One that he liked to have function all on its own, apparently, and without any oversight or aid.

"My mother gave away a child before she married my father," Matteo Combe, her boss, had told her one fine day several weeks back in his usual grave tone.

Lauren, like everyone else who had been in the vicinity of a tabloid in a checkout line over the past forty years, knew all about her boss's parents. And she knew more than most, having spent the bulk of her career working for Matteo. Beautiful, beloved Alexandrina San Giacomo, aristocratic and indulged, had defied reason and her snooty Venetian heritage when she'd married rich but decidedly unpolished Eddie Combe, whose ancestors had carved their way out of the mills of Northern England—often with their fists. Their love story had caused scandals, their turbulent marriage had been the subject of endless speculation and their deaths within weeks of each other had caused even more commotion.

But there had never been the faintest whisper of an illegitimate son.

Lauren had not needed to be told that once

this came out—and it would, because things like this always came out eventually—it wouldn't be whispers they'd have to be worried about. It would be the all-out baying of the tabloid wolves.

"I want you to find him," Matteo had told her, as if he was asking her to fetch him a coffee. "I cannot begin to imagine what his situation is, but I need him media-ready and, if at all possible, compliant."

"Your long-lost brother. Whom you have never met. Who may, for all you know, loathe you and your mother and all other things San Giacomo on principle alone. This is who you think might decide to comply with your wishes."

"I have faith in you," Matteo had replied.

And Lauren had excused that insanity almost in that same instant, because the man had so much on his plate. His parents had died, one after the next. His fluffy-headed younger sister had gone and gotten herself pregnant, a state of affairs that had caused Matteo to take a swing at the father of her baby. A perfectly reasonable reaction, to Lauren's mind—but unfortunately, Matteo had taken said swing at his father's funeral.

The punch he'd landed on Prince Ares of Atilia had been endlessly photographed and videoed by the assorted paparazzi and not a few of the guests, and the company's board of directors had taken it as an opportunity to move against him. Matteo had been forced to subject himself to an anger management specialist who was no ally, and it was entirely possible the board would succeed in removing him should the specialist's report be unflattering.

Of course, Lauren excused him.

"Do you ever *not* excuse him?" her flatmate Mary had asked idly without looking up from her mobile while Lauren had dashed about on her way out the morning she'd left London.

"He's an important and very busy man, Mary."

"As you are always on hand to remind us."

The only reason Lauren hadn't leaped into *that* fray, she told herself now as she stormed along the dirt path toward God knew where, was because good flatmates were hard to find, and Mary's obsession with keeping in touch with her thirty thousand best friends in all corners of the globe on all forms of social media at all times meant she spent most of her time locked in her room obsessing over photo filters and silly voices. Which left the flat to Lauren on the odd occasions she was actually there to enjoy it.

Besides, a small voice inside her that she would have listed as a grievance if she allowed herself to acknowledge it, *she wasn't wrong, was she?*

But Lauren was here to carry out Matteo's wishes, not question her allegiance to him.

Today her pair of typically frothy heels— with studs and spikes and a dash of whimsy because she didn't own a pair of sensible shoes appropriate for mud and woods and never would—were making this unplanned trek through the Hungarian woods even more unpleasant than she'd imagined it would be, and Lauren's imagination was quite vivid. She glared down at her feet, pulled her red wrap tighter around her, thought a few unkind thoughts about her boss she would never utter out loud and kept to the path.

The correct Dominik James had not been easy to find.

There had been almost no information to go on aside from what few details Matteo's mother had provided in her will. Lauren had started with the solicitor who had put Alexandrina's last will and testament together, a canny old man better used to handling the affairs of aristocrats than entertaining the questions of staff. He had peered at her over glasses she wasn't entirely convinced he needed, straight down his nose as he'd assured her that had there been any more pertinent information, he would have included it.

Lauren somehow doubted it.

While Matteo was off tending to his anger management sessions with the future of Combe Industries hanging in the balance, Lauren had launched herself into a research frenzy. The facts were distressingly simple. Alexandrina, heiress to the great San Giacomo fortune, known throughout the world as yet another poor little rich girl, had become pregnant when she was barely fifteen, thanks to a decidedly unsuitable older boy she shouldn't have met in the first place. The family had discovered her pregnancy when she'd been unable to keep hiding it and had transferred her from the convent school she had been attending to one significantly more draconian.

The baby had been born in the summer when Alexandrina was sixteen, spirited away by the church, and Alexandrina had returned to her society life come fall as if nothing had happened. As far as Lauren could tell, she had never mentioned her first son again until she'd made provisions for him in her will.

To my firstborn son, Dominik James, taken from me when I was little more than a child myself, I leave one third of my fortune and worldly goods.

The name itself was a clue. James, it turned out, was an Anglicized version of Giacomo. Lauren tracked all the Dominik Jameses of a certain age she could find, eventually settling on two possibilities. The first she'd dismissed after she found his notably non–San Giacomo DNA profile on one of those ancestry websites. Which left only the other.

The remaining Dominik James had been raised in a series of Catholic orphanages in Italy before running off to Spain. There he'd spent his adolescence, moving from village to village in a manner Lauren could only describe as itinerant. He had joined the Italian Army in his twenties, then disappeared after his discharge. He'd emerged recently to do a stint at university, but had thereafter receded from public view once more.

It had taken some doing, but Lauren had laboriously tracked him down into this gnarled, remote stretch of Hungarian forest—which

Matteo had informed her, after all her work, was the single notation made in the paper version of Alexandrina's will found among Matteo's father's possessions.

"That was what my father wrote on his copy of my mother's will," Matteo had said cheerfully. *Cheerfully*, as if it didn't occur to him that knowing the correct Dominik James was in Hungary might have been information Lauren could have used earlier.

She didn't say that, of course. She'd thanked him.

Matteo's father might have made notes on Alexandrina's will, but he'd clearly had no intention of finding the illegitimate child his wife had given away long before he'd met her. Which meant it was left to Lauren to not only make this trek to locate Dominik James in the first place, but also potentially to break the news of his parentage to him. Here.

In these woods that loomed all about her, foreign and imposing, and more properly belonged in a fairy tale.

Good thing Lauren didn't believe in fairy tales.

She adjusted her red wrap again, pulling it tighter around her to ward off the chill.

It was spring, though there was no way of telling down here on the forest floor. The trees were thick and tall and blocked out the daylight. The shadows were intense, creeping this way and that and making her feel... restless.

Or possibly it wasn't shadows cast by tree branches that were making her feel one way or another, she told herself tartly as she willed her ankles not to roll or her sharp heels to snap off. Perhaps it was the fact that she was here in the first place. Or the fact that when she'd told the innkeeper in this remote mountain town that she was looking for Dominik James, he'd laughed.

"Good luck with that," he had told her, which she had found remarkably unhelpful. "Some men do not want to be found, miss, and nothing good comes of ignoring their issues."

Out here in these woods, where there were nothing but trees all around and the uneasy sensation that she was both entirely alone and not alone at all, that unhelpful statement felt significantly more ominous.

On and on she walked. She had left the village behind a solid thirty minutes ago, and that was the last she'd seen of anything resembling civilization. She tried to tell herself it was lucky this path didn't go directly up the side of the brooding mountains, but it was hard to think in terms of luck when there was nothing around but dirt. Thick trees. Birds causing commotions in the branches over her head. And the kind of crackling sounds that assured her that just because she couldn't see any wildlife, it didn't mean it wasn't there.

Watching. Waiting.

Lauren shuddered. Then told herself she was being ridiculous as she rounded another curve in her path, and that was when she saw it.

At first, she wasn't sure if this was the wooded, leafy version of a desert mirage—not that she'd experienced such a thing, as there were no deserts in London. But the closer she got, the more she could see that her eyes were not deceiving her, after all. There was a rustic sort of structure peeking through the trees, tucked away in a clearing.

Lauren drew closer, slowing her steps as the path led her directly toward the edge of the clearing. All she'd wanted this whole walk was a break from the encroaching forest, but now that there was a clearing, she found it made her nervous.

But Lauren didn't believe in nerves, so she ignored the sensation and frowned at the structure before her. It was a cottage. Hewn from wood, logs interlocking and tidy. There was smoke curling up from its chimney, and there was absolutely no reason that a dedicated city dweller like Lauren should feel something clutch inside her at the sight. As if she'd spent her entire life wandering around without knowing it, half-lost in forests of wood and concrete alike, looking for a cozy little home exactly like this one.

That was ridiculous, of course. Lauren rubbed at her chest without entirely meaning to, as if she could do something about the ache there. She didn't believe in fairy tales, but she'd read them. And if any good had ever come from seemingly perfect cottages slapped down in the middle of dangerous forests, well. She couldn't remember that story. Usually, an enchanted cottage led straight to witches and curses and wolves baring their teeth—

But that was when she noticed that the porch in front of the cottage wasn't empty as she'd thought at first glance. That one of the shadows there was a man.

And he was staring straight at her.

Her heart did something acrobatic and astonishing inside her chest, and she had the strangest notion that if she surrendered to it, it could topple her straight to the ground. Right there on that edge where the forest fought to take back the clearing.

But Lauren had no intention of crumpling.

No matter who was lurking about, staring at her.

"Mr. Dominik James?" she asked briskly, making her voice as crisp and clear as possible and projecting it across the clearing as if she wasn't the slightest bit unnerved, because she shouldn't have been.

Though she was standing stock-still, she couldn't help but notice. As if her legs were not necessarily as convinced as she was that she could continue to remain upright. Especially while her heart kept up its racket and ache.

The man moved, stepping out from the shadow of the porch into the sunlight that filled the clearing but somehow did nothing to push back the inky darkness of the forest.

It only made her heart carry on even worse.

He was tall. Much too tall, with the kind of broad shoulders that made her palms itch to…do things she refused to let herself imagine. His hair was dark and thick, worn carelessly and much too long for her tastes, but it seemed to make his strong, bold jaw more prominent somehow. His mouth was flat and unsmiling, yet was lush enough to make her stomach flip around inside her. He was dressed simply, in a long-sleeved shirt that clung to the hard planes of his chest, dark trousers that made her far too aware of his powerful thighs, and boots that looked as if they'd been chosen for their utility rather than their aesthetics.

But it was his eyes that made everything inside Lauren ring with alarm. Or maybe it was awareness.

Because they were gray. Gray like storms, just like Matteo's.

San Giacomo gray, Lauren thought, just like Alexandrina's had been. Famously.

She didn't need him to identify himself. She had no doubt whatsoever that she was looking at the lost San Giacomo heir. And she couldn't have said why all the tiny hairs on the back of her neck stood up straight as if in foreboding.

She willed herself to forge on.

"My name is Lauren Clarke," she informed him, trying to remember that she was meant to be efficient. Not…whatever she was right now, with all these strange sensations swishing around inside her. "I work for Matteo Combe, president and CEO of Combe Industries. If you are somehow unfamiliar with Mr. Combe, he is, among other things, the

eldest son of the late Alexandrina San Giacomo Combe. I have reason to believe that
Alexandrina was also your mother."

She had practiced that. She had turned the
words over and over in her head, then gone
so far as to practice them in the mirror this
morning in her little room at the inn. Because
there was no point hemming and hawing and
beating around the bush. Best to rip the plas-
ter off and dive straight in, so they could get
to the point as quickly as possible.

She'd expected any number of responses to
her little speech. Maybe he would deny the
claim. Maybe he would launch into bluster,
or order her away. She'd worked out contingency plans for all possible scenarios—

But the man in front of her didn't say a
word.

He roamed toward her, forcing her to notice the way he moved. It was more liquid
than it ought to have been. A kind of lethal
grace, given how big he was, and she found
herself holding her breath.

The closer he came, the more she could see
the expression on his face, in his eyes, that
struck her as a kind of sardonic amusement.

She hadn't made any contingency plan for
that.

"When Mrs. Combe passed recently, she

made provisions for you in her will," Lauren forced herself to continue. "My employer intends to honor his mother's wishes, Mr. James. He has sent me here to start that process."

The man still didn't speak. He slowed when he was face-to-face with Lauren, but all he did was study her. His gaze moved all over her in a way that struck her as almost unbearably intimate, and she could feel the flush that overtook her in reaction.

As if he had his hands all over her body. As if he was testing the smoothness of the hair she'd swept back into a low ponytail. Or the thickness of the bright red wool wrap she wore to ward off the chill of flights and Hungarian forests alike. Down her legs to her pretty, impractical shoes, then back up again.

"Mr. Combe is a man of wealth and consequence." Lauren found it was difficult to maintain her preferred crisp, authoritative tone when this man was so...close. And when he was looking at her as if she were a meal, not a messenger. "I mention this not to suggest that he doesn't wish to honor his commitments to you, because he does. But his stature requires that we proceed with a certain sensitivity. You understand."

She was aware of too many things, all at

once. The man—Dominik, she snapped at herself, because it had to be him—had recently showered. She could see the suggestion of dampness in his hair as it went this way and that, indicating it had a mind of its own. Worse still, she could smell him. The combination of soap and warm, clean, decidedly healthy male.

It made her feel the slightest bit dizzy, and she was sure that was why her heart was careening about inside her chest like a manic drum.

All around them, the forest waited. Not precisely silent, but there was no comforting noise of city life—conversations and traffic and the inevitable sounds of so many humans going about their lives, pretending they were alone—to distract her from this man's curious, penetrating, unequivocally gray glare.

If she believed in nerves, she'd have said hers were going haywire.

"I beg your pardon," Lauren said when it was that or leap away from him and run for it, so unsettled and unsteady did she feel. "Do you speak English? I didn't think to ask."

His stern mouth curled the faintest bit in one corner. As Lauren watched, stricken and frozen for reasons she couldn't begin to explain to herself, he reached across the scant few inches between them.

She thought he was going to put his hand on her—touch her face, or smooth it over her hair, or run one of those bluntly elegant fingers along the length of her neck the way she'd seen in a fanciful romantic movie she refused to admit she'd watched—but he didn't. And she felt the sharpest sense of disappointment in that same instant he found one edge of her wrap, and held it between his fingers.

As if he was testing the wool.

"What are you doing?" Lauren asked, and any hope she'd had of maintaining her businesslike demeanor fled. Her knees were traitorously weak. And her voice didn't sound like her at all. It was much too breathy. Embarrassingly insubstantial.

He was closer than he ought to have been, because she was sure there was no possible way *she* had moved. And there was something about the way he angled his head that made everything inside her shift.

Then go dangerously still.

"A beautiful blonde girl walks into the woods, dressed in little more than a bright, red cloak." His voice was an insinuation. A spell. It made her think of fairy tales again, giving no quarter to her disbelief. It was too smoky, too deep and much too rich, and faintly accented in ways that kicked up terrible wildfires in her blood. And everywhere else. "What did you think would happen?"

Then he dropped his shockingly masculine head to hers, and kissed her.

CHAPTER TWO

HE WAS KISSING HER.

Kissing her, for the love of all that was holy.

Lauren understood it on an intellectual level, but it didn't make sense.

Mostly because what he did with his mouth bore no resemblance to any kiss she had ever heard of or let herself imagine.

He licked his way along her lips, a temptation and a seduction in one, encouraging her to open. To him.

Which of course she wasn't going to do.

Until she did, with a small sound in the back of her throat that made her shudder everywhere else.

And then that wicked temptation of a tongue was inside her mouth—*inside* her—and everything went a little mad.

It was the angle, maybe. His taste, rich and wild. It was the impossible, lazy mastery of the way he kissed her, deepening it, changing it.

When he pulled away, his mouth was still curved.

And Lauren was the one who was shaking.

She assured herself it was temper. Outrage. "You can't just...go about *kissing* people!"

That curve in his mouth deepened. "I will keep that in mind, should any more storybook creatures emerge from my woods."

Lauren was flustered. Her cheeks were too hot and that same heat seemed to slide and melt its way all over her body, making her nipples pinch while between her legs, a kind of slippery need bloomed.

And shamed her. Deeply.

"I am not a storybook creature." The moment she said it, she regretted it. Why was she participating in whatever bizarre delusion this was? But she couldn't seem to stop herself. "Fairy tales aren't real, and even if they were, I would want nothing to do with them."

"That is a terrible shame. What are fairy tales if not a shorthand for all of mankind's temptations? Fantasies. Dark imaginings."

There was no reason that her throat should feel so tight. She didn't need to swallow like that, and she certainly didn't need to be so *aware* of it.

"I'm sure that some people's jobs—or lack thereof—allow them to spend time considering the merit of children's stories," she said in a tone she was well aware was a touch too prissy. But that was the least of her concerns just then, with the brand of his mouth on hers. "But I'm afraid my job is rather more adult."

"Because nothing is more grown-up than doing the bidding of another, of course."

Lauren felt off-kilter, when she never did. Her lips felt swollen, but she refused to lift her fingers to test them. She was afraid it would give him far too much advantage. It would show him her vulnerability, and that was unconscionable.

The fact she had any vulnerability to show in the first place was an outrage.

"Not everyone can live by their wits in a forest hut," she said. Perhaps a bit acerbically.

But if she expected him to glower at that, she was disappointed. Because all he did was stare back at her, that curve in the corner of his mouth, and his eyes gleaming a shade of silver that she felt in all those melting places inside her.

"Your innkeeper told me you were coming." He shifted back only slightly, and she was hyperaware of him in ways that humiliated her further. There was something about the way his body moved. There was something about him. He made her want to lean in closer. He made her want to reach out her hands and—

But of course she didn't do that. She folded her arms across her chest, to hold him off and hold herself together at the same time, and trained her fiercest glare upon him as if that could make all the uncomfortable feelings go away.

"You could have saved yourself the trouble and the walk," he was saying. "I don't want your rich boss and yes, I know who he is. You can rest easy. I'm not interested in him. Or his mother. Or whatever 'provisions' appeared in the wills of overly wealthy people I would likely hate if I'd known them personally."

That felt like a betrayal when it shouldn't have felt like anything. It wasn't personal. She had nothing to do with the Combe and San Giacomo families. She had never been anything but staff, for which she often felt grateful, as there was nothing like exposure to the very wealthy and known to make a person grateful for the things she had—all of which came without the scrutiny and weight of all those legacies.

But the fact this man didn't want his own birthright...rankled. Lauren's lips tingled.

They felt burned, almost, and she could remember the way his mouth had moved on hers so vividly that she could taste him all over again. Bold and unapologetic. Ruthlessly male.

And somehow that all wrapped around itself, became a knot and pulled tight inside her.

"My rich boss is your brother," she pointed out, her voice sharper than it should have been. "This isn't about money. It's about family."

"A very rich family," Dominik agreed. And his gaze was more steel than silver then. "Who didn't want me in the first place. I will pass, I think, on a tender reunion brought about by the caprice of a dead woman."

Her heart lurched when he reached out and took her chin in his hand. She should have slapped him away. She meant to, surely.

But everything was syrupy, thick and slow. And all she could feel was the way he gripped her. The way he held her chin with a kind of certainty that made everything inside her quiver in direct contrast to that firm hold. She'd gone soft straight through. Melting hot. Impossibly...changed.

"I appreciate the taste," he rumbled at her, sardonic and lethal and more than she could bear—but she still didn't pull away from him. "I had no idea such a sharp blonde could taste so sweet."

And he had already turned and started back toward his cabin by the time those words fully penetrated all that odd, internal shaking.

Lauren thought she would hate herself forever for the moisture she could feel in her own eyes, when she hadn't permitted herself furious tears in as long as she could remember.

"Let me make certain I'm getting this straight," she threw at his back, and she certainly *did not* notice how muscled he was, everywhere, or how easy it was to imagine her own hands running down the length of his spine, purely to marvel in the way he was put together. *Certainly not.* "The innkeeper called ahead, which means you knew I was coming. Did he tell you what I was wearing, too? So you could prepare this Red Riding Hood story to tell yourself?"

"If the cloak fits," he said over his shoulder.

"That would make you the Big Bad Wolf, would it not?"

She found herself following him, which couldn't possibly be wise. Marching across that clearing as if he hadn't made her feel so adrift. So shaky.

As if he hadn't kissed her within an inch of her life, but she wasn't thinking about that.

Because she couldn't think about that, or she would think of nothing else.

"There are all kinds of wolves in the forests of Europe." And his voice seemed darker then. Especially when he turned, training that gray gaze of his on her all over again. It had the same effect as before. Looking at him was like staring into a storm. "Big and bad is as good a description as any."

She noticed he didn't answer the question. "Why?"

Lauren stopped a foot or so in front of him. She found her hands on her hips, the wrap falling open. And she hated the part of her that thrilled at the way his gaze tracked over the delicate gold chain at her throat. The silk blouse beneath.

Her breasts that felt heavy and achy, and the nipples that were surely responding to the sudden exposure to colder air. Not him.

She had spent years wearing gloriously girly shoes to remind herself she was a woman, desperately hoping that each day was the day that Matteo would see her as one for a change. He never had. He never would.

And this man made her feel outrageously feminine without even trying.

She told herself what she felt about that was sheer, undiluted outrage, but it was a little too giddy, skidding around and around inside her, for her to believe it.

"Why did I kiss you?" She saw the flash of his teeth, like a smile he thought better of at the last moment, and that didn't make anything happening inside her better. "Because I wanted to, little red. What other reason could there be?"

"Perhaps you kissed me because you're a pig," she replied coolly. "A common affliction in men who feel out of control, I think you'll find."

A kind of dark delight moved over his face.

"I believe you have your fairy tales confused. And in any case, where there are pigs, there is usually also huffing and puffing and, if I am not mistaken, blowing." He tilted that head of his to one side, reminding her in an instant how untamed he was. How outside her experience. "Are you propositioning me?"

She felt a kind of red bonfire ignite inside her, all over her, but she didn't give in to it. She didn't distract herself with images of exactly what he might mean by *blowing*. And how best she could accommodate him like the fairy tale of his choice, right here in this clearing, sinking down on her knees and—

"Very droll," she said instead, before she shamed herself even further. "I'm not at all surprised that a man who lives in a shack in the woods has ample time to sit around, perverting fairy tales to his own ends. But I'm not here for you, Mr. James."

"Call me Dominik." He smiled at her then, but she didn't make the mistake of believing him the least bit affable. Not when that smile made her think of a knife, sharp and deadly. "I would say that Mr. James was my father, but I've never met the man."

"I appreciate this power play of yours," Lauren said, trying a new tactic before she could get off track again, thinking of *knives* and *blowing* and *that kiss*. "I feel very much put in my place, thank you. I would love nothing more than to turn tail and run back to my employer, with tales of the uncivilized hermit in the woods that he'd be better off never recognizing as his long-lost brother. But I'm afraid I can't do that."

"Why not?"

"Because it doesn't matter why you're here in the woods. Whether you're a hermit, a barbarian, an uncivilized lout unfit for human company." She waved one hand, airily, as if she couldn't possibly choose among those things. "If I could track you down, that means others will, as well, and they won't be nearly as pleasant as I am. They will be reporters. Paparazzi. And once they start coming, they will always come. They will surround this cabin and make your life a living hell. That's what they do." She smiled. Sunnily. "It's only a matter of time."

"I spent my entire childhood waiting for people to come," he said softly, after a moment that stretched out between them and made her...edgy. "They never did. You will forgive me if I somehow find it difficult to believe that now, suddenly, I will become of interest to anyone."

"When you were a child you were an illegitimate mistake," Lauren said, making her voice cold to hide that odd yearning inside her that made her wish she could go back in time and save the little boy he'd been from his fate. "That's what Alexandrina San Giacomo's father wrote about you. That's not my description." She hurried to say that last part, something in the still way he watched her making her stomach clench. "Now you are the San Giacomo heir you always should have been. You are a very wealthy man, Mr.

James. More than that, you are part of a long and illustrious family line, stretching back generations."

"You could not be more mistaken," he said in the same soft way that Lauren didn't dare mistake for any kind of weakness. Not when she could see that expression on his face, ruthless and lethal in turn. "I am an orphan. An ex-soldier. And a man who prefers his own company. If I were you, I would hurry back to the man who keeps you on his leash and tell him so." There was a dangerous gleam in his eyes then. "Now, like a good pet. Before I forget how you taste and indulge my temper instead."

Lauren wanted nothing more. If being a pet on Matteo's leash could keep her safe from this man, she wanted it. But that wasn't the task that had been set before her. "I'm afraid I can't do that."

"There is no alternative, little red. I have given you my answer."

Lauren could see he meant that. He had every intention of walking back into this ridiculous cottage in the middle of nowhere, washing his hands of his birthright and pretending no one had found him. She felt a surge of a different kind of emotion at that, and it wasn't one that spoke well of her.

Because *she* wouldn't turn up her nose at the San Giacomo fortune and everything that went along with it. She wouldn't scoff at the notion that maybe she'd been a long-lost heiress all this time. Far better that than the boring reality, which was that both her mother and father had remarried and had sparkly new families they'd always seemed to like a whole lot more than her, the emblem of the bad decisions they'd made together.

They'd tossed her back and forth between them with bad grace and precious little affection, until she'd finally come of age and announced it could stop. The sad truth was that Lauren had expected one of them to argue. Or at least pretend to argue. But neither one of them had bothered.

And she doubted she would mind that *quite* so much if she had aristocratic blood and a sudden fortune to ease the blow.

"Most people would be overjoyed to this news," she managed to say without tripping over her own emotions. "It's a bit like winning the lottery, isn't it? You go along living your life only to discover that all of a sudden, you're a completely different person than the one you thought you were."

"I am exactly who I think I am." And there was something infinitely dangerous beneath his light tone. She could see it in his gaze. "I worked hard to become him. I have no intention of casting him aside because of some dead woman's guilt."

"But I don't—"

"I know who the San Giacomos are," Dominik said shortly. "How could I not? I grew up in Italy in their shadow and I want no part of it. Or them. You can tell your boss that."

"He will only send me back here. Eventually, if you keep refusing me, he will come himself. Is that what you want? The opportunity to tell him to his face how little you want the gift he is giving you?"

Dominik studied her. "Is it a gift? Or is it what I was owed from my birth, yet prevented from claiming?"

"Either way, it's nothing if you lock yourself up in your wood cabin and pretend it isn't happening."

He laughed at that. He didn't fling back his head and let out a belly laugh. He only smiled. A quick sort of smile on an exhale, which only seemed to whet Lauren's appetite for real laughter.

What on earth was happening to her?

"What I don't understand is your zeal," he said, his voice like a dark lick down the length of her spine. And it did her no favors to imagine him doing exactly that, that tongue of his against her flesh, following the flare of her hips with his hands while he... She had to shake herself slightly, hopefully imperceptibly, and frown to focus on him. "I know you have been searching for me. It has taken you weeks, but you have been dogged in your pursuit. If it occurred to you at any point that I did not wish to be found, you did not let that give you the slightest bit of pause. And now you have come here. Uninvited."

"If you knew I was searching for you—" and she would have to think about what that meant, because that suggested a level of sophistication the wood cabin far out in these trees did not "—why didn't you reach out yourself?"

"Nobody sets himself apart from the world in a tiny cottage in a forest in Hungary if they wish to have visitors. Much less unannounced visitors." His smile was that knife again, a sharp, dangerous blade. "But here you are."

"I'm very good at my job." Lauren lifted her chin. "Remarkably good, in fact. When I'm given a task to complete, I complete it."

"He says jump and you aim for the moon,"

Dominik said softly. And she could hear the insult in it. It sent another flush of something like shame, splashing all over her, and she didn't understand it. She didn't understand any of this.

"I'm a personal assistant, Mr. James. That means I assist my employer in whatever it is he needs. It is the nature of the position. Not a character flaw."

"Let me tell you what I know of your employer," Dominik said, and his voice went lazy as if he was playing. But she couldn't quite believe he was. Or that he ever did, come to that. "He is a disgrace, is he not? A man so enamored of this family you have come all this way to make me a part of that he punched his sister's lover in the face at their father's funeral. What a paragon! I cannot imagine why I have no interest involving myself with such people."

Lauren really was good at her job. She had to remind herself of that at the moment, but it didn't make it any less true. She pulled in a breath, then let it out slowly, trying to understand what was actually happening here.

That this man had a grudge against the people who had given him to an orphanage was clear. Understandable, even. She supposed it was possible that he wasn't turning his nose up at what Matteo was offering so much as the very idea that an offer was being made at all, all these years too late to matter. She could understand that, too, having spent far more hours than she cared to admit imagining scenarios in which her parents begged for her time—so she could refuse them and sweep off somewhere.

And if she had been a man sent to find him, she supposed Dominik would have found a different way to get under her skin the same way he would any emissary sent from those who had abandoned him. All his talk of kissing and fairy tales was just more misdirection. Game-playing. Like all the scenarios she'd played out in her head about her parents.

She had to assume that his refusal to involve himself with the San Giacomos was motivated by hurt feelings. But if she knew one thing about men—no matter how powerful, wealthy or seemingly impervious—it was that all of them responded to hurt feelings as if the feelings themselves were an attack. And anyone in the vicinity was a collaborator.

"I appreciate your position, Dominik," she said, trying to sound conciliatory. Sweet, even, since he was the first person alive who'd ever called her that. "I really do. But I still want to restore you to your family. What do I have to do to make that happen?"

"First, you go wandering around the forbidding woods in a red cloak." Dominik shook his head, making a faint *tsk*-ing sound. "Then you let the Big Bad Wolf find out how you taste. Now an open-ended offer? My, my. What big eyes you have, little red."

There was no reason she should shiver at that, as if he was making predictions instead of taking part in this same extended game that she had already given too much of her time and attention.

But the woods were all around them. The breeze whispered through the trees, and the village with all its people was far, far away from here.

And he'd already kissed her.

What, exactly, are you offering him? she asked herself.

But she had no answer.

Looking at Dominik James made Lauren feel as if she didn't know herself at all. It made her feel like her body belonged to someone else, shivery and nervous. It made her tongue feel as if it no longer worked the way it should. She didn't like it at all. She didn't like *him*, she told herself.

But she didn't turn on her heel and leave, either.

"There must be something that could convince you to come back to London and take your rightful place as a member of the San Giacomo family," she said, trying to sound reasonable. Calmly rational. "It's clearly not money, or you would have jumped at the chance to access your own fortune."

He shrugged. "You cannot tempt me with that kind of power."

"Because, of course, you prefer to play power games like this. Where you pretend you have no interest in power, all the while using what power you do have to do the exact opposite of anything asked of you."

It was possible she shouldn't have said that, she reflected in some panic as his gaze narrowed on her in a way that made her...shake, deep inside.

But if she expected him to shout or issue threats, he didn't. He only studied her in that way for another moment, then grinned. Slowly.

A sharp blade of a grin that made her stop breathing, even as it boded ill.

For her. For the heart careening around and battering her ribs.

For all the things she wanted to pretend

she didn't feel, like a thick, consuming heat inside her.

"By all means, little red," he said, his voice low. "Come inside. Sit by my fire. Convince me, if you can."

CHAPTER THREE

DOMINIK JAMES HAD spent his entire life looking for his place in the world.

They had told him his parents were dead. That he was an orphan in truth, and he had believed that. At first. It certainly explained his circumstances in life, and as a child, he'd liked explanations that made sense of the orphanage he called home.

But when he was ten, the meanest of the nuns had dropped a different truth on him when she'd caught him in some or other mischief.

Your mother didn't want you, she had told him. *And who could blame her with you such a dirty, nasty sneak of a boy. Who could want you?*

Who indeed? Dominik had spent the next ten years proving to everyone's satisfaction that his mother, whoever she was, had been perfectly justified in ridding herself of him.

He had lived down to any and all expectations. He'd run away from the orphanage and found himself in Spain, roaming where he pleased and stealing what he needed to live. He'd considered that happiness compared to the nuns' version of corporal punishment mixed in with vicious piety.

He had eventually gone back to Italy and joined the army, more to punish himself than as any display of latent patriotism. He'd hoped that he would be sent off to some terrible war where he could die in service to Italy rather than from his own nihilistic urges. He certainly hadn't expected to find discipline instead. Respect. A place in the world, and the tools to make himself the kind of man who deserved that place.

He had given Italy his twenties. After he left the service, he'd spent years doing what the army had taught him on a private civilian level until he'd gotten restless. He'd then sold the security company he'd built for a tidy fortune.

Left to his own devices as a grown man with means, he had bettered himself significantly. He had gotten a degree to expand his thinking. His mind. And, not inconsiderably, to make sure he could manage his newfound fortune the way he wanted to do.

He didn't need his long-lost family's money. He had his own. The computer security company he had built up almost by accident had made him a very wealthy man. Selling it had made him a billionaire. And he'd enjoyed building on that foundation ever since, expanding his financial reach as he pleased.

He just happened to enjoy pretending he was a hermit in the Hungarian woods, because he could. And because, in truth, he liked to keep a wall or a forest between him and whatever else was out there. He liked to stay arm's length, at the very least, from the world that had always treated him with such indifference. The world that had made him nothing but bright with rage and sharp with fury, even when he was making it his.

Dominik preferred cool shadows and quiet trees these days. The comfort of his own company. Nothing brighter than the sun as it filtered down through the trees, and no fury at all.

Sharp-edged blondes with eyes like caramel who tasted like magic made him…greedy and hot. It made him feel like a long-lost version of himself that he had never meant to see resurrected.

He should have sent her away at once.

Instead, he'd invited her in.

She walked in front of him, those absurd and absurdly loud shoes of hers making it clear that she was not the sort of woman who ever expected to sneak up on a person, especially when they hit the wood of his porch. And he regretted letting her precede him almost at once, because while the cloak she wore—so bright and red it was almost as if she was having a joke at his expense— hid most of that lush and lean body from his view, it couldn't conceal the way her hips swung back and forth like a metronome.

Dominik had never been so interested in keeping the beat before in his life. He couldn't look away. Then again, he didn't try that hard.

When she got to his front door, a heavy wood that he'd fashioned himself with iron accents because perhaps he really had always thought of himself as the Big Bad Wolf, he reached past her. He pushed the door open with the flat of one hand, inviting her in.

But that was a mistake, too.

Because he had already tasted her, and leaning in close made him...needy. He wanted his mouth right there on the nape of her neck. He wanted his hands on the full breasts he'd glimpsed beneath that sheer blouse she wore. He wanted to bury his face between her legs, then lose himself completely in all her sweet heat.

Instead, all he did was hold the door for her. Meekly, as if he was some other man. Someone tamed. Civilized.

A hermit in a hut, just as he pretended to be.

He watched her walk inside, noting how stiff and straight she held herself as if she was terrified that something might leap out at her. But this cabin had been made to Dominik's precise specifications. It existed to be cozy. Homey.

It was the retreat he had never had as a boy, and he had absolutely no idea why he had allowed this particular woman to come inside. When no one else ever had.

He wasn't sure he wanted to think about that too closely.

"This is a bit of a shock," she said into the silence that stretched taut between them, her gaze moving from the thick rugs on the floor to the deep leather chairs before the fire. "I expected something more like a hovel, if I'm honest."

"A hovel."

"I mean no disrespect," she said, which he thought was a lie. She did that thing with her hand again, waving at him in a manner he could only call dismissive. It was…new, at least. "No one really expects a long-haired hermit to live in any kind of splendor, do they?"

"I am already regretting my hospitality," Dominik murmured.

He looked around at the cabin, trying to see it through the eyes of someone like Lauren, all urban chic and London snootiness. He knew the type, of course, though he'd gone to some lengths to distance himself from such people. The shoes were a dead giveaway. Expensive and pointless, because they were a statement. She wanted everyone who saw them to wonder how she walked in them, or wonder how much they cost, or drift away in a sea of their own jealousy.

Dominik merely wondered what it said about her that her primary form of expression was her shoes.

He also wondered what she was gleaning about him from this cabin that was his only real home. He didn't know what she saw, only what he'd intended. The soaring high ceilings, because he had long since grown tired of stooping and making himself fit into spaces not meant for him. The warm rugs, because he was tired of being cold and uncomfortable. The sense of airiness that made the cottage feel as if it was twice its actual size, because he had done his time in huts and hovels and he wasn't going back. The main room boasted a stone fireplace on one end and his efficient kitchen on the other, and he'd fashioned a bedchamber that matched it in size, outfitted with a bed that could fit two of him—because he never forgot those tiny cots he'd had to pretend to be grateful for in the orphanage.

"It's actually quite lovely," she said after a moment, a note of reluctant surprise in her voice. "Very...comfortable, yet male."

Dominik jerked his chin toward one of the heavy chairs that sat before his fire. Why there were two, he would never know, since he never had guests. But when he'd imagined the perfect cabin and the fireplace that would dominate it, he had always envisioned two cozy leather chairs, just like these. So here they were.

And he had the strangest sensation, as Lauren went and settled herself into one of them, that he had anticipated this moment. It was almost as if the chair had been waiting for her all this time.

He shook that off, not sure where such a

fanciful notion had come from. But very sure that he didn't like it. At all.

He dropped into the chair opposite hers, and lounged there, doing absolutely nothing at all to accommodate her when he let his long legs take over the space between them. He watched her swallow, as if her throat was dry, and he could have offered her a drink.

But he didn't.

"I thought you intended to convince me to do your bidding," he said after a moment, when the air between them seemed to get thick. Fraught. Filled with premonition and meaning, when he wanted neither. "Perhaps things are different where you're from, but I would not begin an attempt at persuasion by insulting the very person I most wanted to come around to my way of thinking. Your mileage may vary, of course."

She blinked at him, and it was almost as if she'd forgotten why they were there. She shrugged out of that wrap at last, then folded her hands in her lap, and Dominik let his gaze fall all over her. Greedily. As if he'd never seen a woman before in all his days.

She was sweet and stacked, curvy in all the right places. Her hair gleamed like gold in the firelight, the sleek ponytail at her nape pulled forward over one shoulder. There was a hint of real gold at her throat, precisely where he wanted to use his teeth—gently, so gently, until she shuddered. Her breasts begged for a man's hands and his face between them, and it would take so little. He could shift forward, onto his knees, and take her in hand that easily.

He entertained a few delicious images of himself doing just that.

And she didn't exactly help matters when she pulled that plump lower lip of hers between her teeth, the way he'd like to do.

But Dominik merely sank deeper into his chair, propped his head up with his fist, and ignored the demands of the hardest, greediest part of him as he gazed at her.

"I would be delighted to persuade you," she said, and did he imagine a certain huskiness in her voice? He didn't think he did. "I expected to walk in here and find you living on a pallet on the floor. But you clearly like your creature comforts. That tells me that while you might like your solitude, you aren't exactly hiding from the world. Or not completely. So what would it take to convince you to step back into it?"

"You have yet to explain to me why that is something I should want, much less consider doing."

"You could buy a hundred cabins and litter them about all the forests of Europe, for a start."

He lifted one shoulder, then let it fall. "I already have a cabin."

And properties across the globe, but he didn't mention that.

"You could outfit this cabin in style," she suggested brightly. "Make it modern and accessible. Imagine the opportunities!"

"I never claimed to live off the grid, did I? I believe you are the one who seems to think this cabin belongs in the Stone Age. I assure you, I have as much access to the modern world as I require."

Not to mention his other little shack that wasn't a shack at all, set farther up the mountainside and outfitted with the very latest in satellite technology. But that was yet another thing that could remain his little secret.

"You could buy yourself anything you wanted."

"All you have to offer me is money," he said after a moment. "I already told you, I have my own. But the fact that you continue to focus on it tells me a great deal about you, I think. Does this brother of mine not pay you well?"

She stiffened at that, and a crease appeared

between her brows. "Mr. Combe has always been remarkably generous to me."

He found the color on her cheeks…interesting. "I cannot tell if that means he does or does not pay you what you deserve. What's the going rate for the kind of loyalty that would lead a woman clearly uncomfortable with the outdoors to march off into the forest primeval, deep into the very lair of a dangerous stranger?"

Her chin tipped up at that, which he should not have found as fascinating as he did. "I fail to see how my salary is your business."

"You have made anything and everything my business by delivering yourself to my door." And if he was overly intrigued by her, to the point his fingers itched with the need to touch her all over that curvy body until she sounded significantly less cool, that was his burden to carry. "Why don't you tell me why you're really here?"

The color on her cheeks darkened. The crease between her brows deepened. And it shouldn't have been possible to sit any straighter in that chair, but she managed it.

"I have already told you why I'm here, Mr. James."

"I'm sure they told you in the village that I come in at least once a week for supplies. You could have waited for me there, surrounded by creature comforts and room service. There was no need at all to walk through the woods to find me, particularly not in those shoes."

She looked almost smug then. As if he'd failed some kind of test.

"You don't need to concern yourself with my shoes," she said, and crossed her legs, which had the immediate effect of drawing his attention to the shoes in question. Just as she'd intended, he assumed. "I find them remarkably comfortable, actually."

"That you find them comfortable, or want me to think you do, doesn't mean they are. And it certainly doesn't make them practical for a brisk hike on a dirt path."

That gaze of hers was the color of a sweet, sticky dessert, and he wanted to indulge. Oh, how he wanted to indulge. Especially when her eyes flashed at him, once again letting him know that she felt superior to him.

Little did she know, he found that entertaining.

Even as it made him harder.

"In my experience, anyone who is concerned with the practicality of my footwear is casting about in desperation for some way to discount what I have to say," she told him. "Focus on my shoes and we can make sweeping generalizations about what sort of person I am, correct? Here's a little secret. I like pretty shoes. They don't say anything about me except that."

Dominik grinned, taking his time with it and enjoying it when she swallowed. Hard.

"Let me hasten to assure you that I'm in no way desperate. And I would love nothing more than to discount what you say, but you have said very little." He held her gaze. "Make your case, if you can. Explain to me why I should leave the comfort of my home to embrace this family who have ignored me for a lifetime already. I'm assuming it would be convenient for them in some way. But you'll understand that's not a compelling argument for me."

"I already told you. The paparazzi—"

He shook his head. "I think we both know that it is not I who would dislike it if your reporters found me here. I am perfectly content to deal with trespassers in my own way." He could see by the way her lips pressed together that she was imagining exactly how he might handle trespassers, and grinned wider. "But this rich boss of yours would not care for the exposure, I imagine. Is that not why you have made your way here, after searching for me so diligently? To convince me that his sudden, surpassing concern for my privacy is a genuine display of heretofore unknown brotherly love rather than his own self-interest?"

"Mr. Combe was unaware that he had a brother until recently," she replied, but her voice had gone cool. Careful, perhaps. "If anything should convince you about his intentions, it should be the fact that he reached out to find you as soon as he knew you existed."

"I must remember to applaud."

She didn't sigh or roll her eyes at that, though the tightness of her smile suggested both nonetheless. "Mr. Combe—"

"Little red. Please. What did you imagine I meant when I asked you to convince me? I've already had my mouth on you. Do you really think I invited you in here for a lecture?"

He didn't know what he expected. Outrage, perhaps. Righteous indignation, then a huffy flounce out of the cabin and out of his life. That was what he wanted, he assured himself.

Because her being here was an intrusion. He'd invited her in to make certain she'd never come back.

Of course you did, a sardonic voice inside him chimed in.

But Lauren wasn't flouncing away in high dudgeon. Instead, she stared back at him with a dumbfounded expression on her face. Not as if she was offended by his suggestion. But more as if...such a thing had never occurred to her.

"I beg your pardon. Is this some kind of cultural divide I'm unfamiliar with? Or do you simply inject sex into conversations whenever you get bored?"

"Whenever possible."

She laughed, and what surprised him was that it sounded real. Not part of this game at all.

"You're wasting your time with me." Her smile was bland. But there was a challenge in her gaze, he thought. "I regret to tell you, as I have told every man before you who imagined they could get to my boss through me, that I have no sexual impulses."

If she had pulled a grenade out of her pocket and lobbed it onto the floor between them, Dominik could not have been more surprised.

He could not possibly have heard her correctly. "What did you just say?"

There before him, his very own Little Red Riding Hood...relaxed back against the leather of her armchair. Something he also would have thought impossible moments before. And when she smiled, she looked like nothing so much as an oversatisfied cat.

"I'm not a sexual person," she told him, and Dominik was sure he wasn't mistaking the relish in her voice. It was at odds with the sheen of something a whole lot like vulnerability in her gaze, reminding him of how she'd melted into his kiss. "It's a spectrum, isn't it? Some people's whole lives are completely taken over by the endless drive for sex, but not me. I've never understood all the fuss, to be honest."

He was half convinced he'd gone slack-jawed in astonishment, but he couldn't seem to snap out of it long enough to check. Not when she was sitting there talking such absolute nonsense with an expression that suggested to him that she, at least, believed every word she was saying.

Or, if he looked closer, *wanted* to believe it, anyway.

"You are aware that a kiss is a sexual act, are you not?"

"I've kissed before," Lauren said, and even shook her head at him, wrinkling up her nose as if he was…silly. Him. *Silly.* "I experimented with kissing when I was at university. As you do. That's how I know that it isn't for me."

"You experimented," he repeated as if that would make sense of what she was saying with such astonishing confidence—though, again, when he looked closer he was almost sure it was an act. Did he merely want it to be? "With kissing."

"As I said, there are all sorts. Not everyone is consumed with the urge to flail about naked. Not that there's anything wrong with that, but some of us have other things to think about." Her expression turned virtuous and Dominik was sure, then, that while she might believe what she was saying, he'd... rocked her foundations. She was overselling it. "More important things."

"And what, dare I ask, is it that consumes your thoughts if not...flailing?"

"You've made quite a few references to my being at Mr. Combe's bidding, but I take my job very seriously. It requires dedication. Focus and energy. I couldn't possibly siphon all of that off into all that trawling about from pub to pub every night, all to..."

"Flail. Naked."

"Exactly."

Dominik knew two things then as surely as he knew himself, his own capabilities and the fact she was lying about her own sexuality. One, if he wasn't misunderstanding what she

was telling him, his sharp, majestically shoed
and caramel-eyed blonde was a virgin. And
two, that possibility made him hard.

Very nearly desperately so.

Because he already knew how she tasted.
He'd heard the noises she'd made when he
kissed her, and no matter what she told herself and was trying to tell him now, he did not
believe that she had been unaffected.

He knew otherwise, in fact, as surely as he
knew his own name.

"I can see how you're looking at me," Lauren said. She was still entirely too relaxed,
to his way of thinking, leaning back in the
leather chair as if she owned it. Clearly certain that she was in total control of this conversation. And him. "I don't understand why
men take this as such a challenge."

Dominik's mouth curved. "Do you not?"

It was her turn to shrug. "I'm perfectly
comfortable with who I am."

"Obviously." He settled back against his
chair until he mirrored her. And for a long
moment, every second of which he could feel
in the place where he was hardest, he simply…studied her. Until her smile faded and
she looked a whole lot less *certain*. "For refer-
ence, little red, people who are perfectly comfortable with themselves rarely mentioned

their sexuality at all, much less bludgeon others over the head with it."

"Oh, I see." Her smile was bland again, and this time, distinctly pitying besides, though he could see the uncertainty she tried to hide. "You're upset because you think I'm saying this because I didn't like your kiss. Don't worry, Mr. James. I don't like any kissing. Not just yours."

"Of the two of us sitting here, Lauren," he said, enjoying the taste of her name in his mouth and the faint tremor in her sweet lower lip that told him the truths she couldn't, "I am the one who is actually comfortable with himself. Not to mention fully aware. I know exactly how much you liked my kiss without you needing to tell me all these stories."

"I'm glad to hear it." Her chin tipped up again, her eyes flashing as if that could hide the glint of doubt there. "I've seen this a thousand times before, you know. First, you will proposition me. Then you'll throw a temper tantrum when I decline your kind offer to see what I'm missing, with you as selfless guide. It's always the same old story."

"Is it? Why don't you tell it to me?"

She waved that hand of hers again. "You will want to kiss me, certain that a mere touch of your lips will awaken me to the joys of the flesh. It won't work, it's already failed to awaken me to anything, but you won't believe me. I can see you already don't believe me." She had the gall to try to look bored. "And if it's all the same to you, I'd rather fast-forward straight through that same old song and dance. It's tedious."

"If you insist." He found himself stroking his jaw with his fingers, because he knew that if he reached over to put them on her, she would take it as evidence of this theory of hers. This *song and dance*. No matter how much she liked it. "And what is on the other side? Once we're finished with all this fast-forwarding?"

"Why, business, of course. What else?"

"But in this case, little red, your business and mine are the same. Aren't you here to tempt me out of my humble cabin and into the great, wide world?"

"I am. All you need to do is name your price."

And Dominik was not an impulsive man. Not anymore. He had learned his lesson, time and again, in his misspent youth.

But there was something about this woman that got to him. She was still smiling at him in that pitying way when he'd already tasted her. When he knew better. He couldn't tell if she was lying to herself as well as him, but try as he might, he couldn't think of a single good reason to deny himself.

Not when Lauren Clarke was the most entertainment he'd had in ages.

And Dominik was no longer in the army. He no longer ran his security company. If he wanted to live his life in pursuit of his own amusement, he could now.

Even if it meant involving himself with the blood relations he had located when he was still in the army, but had never seen any reason to contact.

Because like hell would he go begging for scraps.

"You must let me kiss you whenever I wish," he said, keeping his voice mild so she wouldn't see that driving need for her inside him, greedy and focused. "That's it. That is my price. Agree and I will go wherever you wish for me to go and do whatever you wish me to do."

"Don't be ridiculous."

He could tell she thought he was kidding, because she didn't bother to sit up straight. Her cheeks didn't flush, and she was still smiling at him as if he was a fool. He felt like one. But that didn't make him want to take back what he'd said.

Especially when he could see the truth all over her, where she couldn't smile it away.

"This fairy tale obsession of yours has gone too far, I think. Let's return to the real world, which I understand is hard out here in an enchanted cottage in the deep, dark woods."

"The first thing you will learn about me is that I'm never ridiculous," Dominik told her, his voice low. "And when I make a promise, I keep it. Will you? You must let me kiss you whenever I like. However I like. This is a simple request, surely. Particularly for a person such as you who doesn't care one way or the other about kissing."

"I already told you, I know how this goes." She'd lost that smile, and was frowning at him then. "You say *kissing*, but that's not what you mean. It always goes further. There's always a hand."

"I do have a hand, yes. Two, in fact. You've caught me."

"One way or another it always leads back to the same discussion. When we can just have it now." She shook her head. "I'm just not sexual. That's the beginning and the end of it."

"Marvelous. Neither am I, by your definition." Dominik gazed at her, and hoped he didn't look as wolfish as he felt. "Let's be nonsexual together."

She blinked at him, then frowned all the more. "I don't think…"

"We can make rules, if you like." It was his turn to smile, and so he did, all the better to beguile her with. "Rule number one, as discussed, you must allow me to kiss you at my whim. Rule number two, when you no longer wish me to kiss you, you will tell me to stop. That's it. That's all I want."

"But…" Her voice was faint. He counted that as a victory.

"And in return for this, little red, I will trot back to England on your boss's leash and perform the role of long-lost brother to his satisfaction. What will that entail, do you think? Will it be acts of fealty in public view? Or will it simply be an appropriate haircut, the better to blend with the stodgy aristocracy?"

She looked bewildered for a moment, and if Dominik had ever had the slightest inkling to imagine himself a good man—which he hadn't—he knew better then. Because he liked it. He liked her off balance, those soft lips parting and her eyes dazed as if she hardly knew what to do with herself.

Oh, yes, he liked it a great deal.

"I don't understand why, when you could

have anything in the world, you would ask for...a kiss."

He could feel the edge in his own smile then. "You cannot buy me, Lauren. But you can kiss me."

She looked dubious, but then, after a moment or two, she appeared to be considering it.

Which Dominik felt like her hands all over his body, skin to skin.

"How long do you imagine this arrangement will go on?" she asked.

He shrugged. "As long as your Mr. Combe requires I remain in his spotlight, I suppose."

"And you give me your word that you will stop when I tell you to."

"I would not be much of a man if I did not," he said, evenly. "There are words to describe those who disregard such clear instructions, but *man* is not among them."

"All you want from the news that you're one of the richest men alive is a kiss," she said after another moment, as if she was selecting each word with care. "And I suppose you can't get much kissing out here in the middle of nowhere, so fair enough, if that's what you like. But why would you choose me?"

Dominik restrained himself—barely—from allowing his very healthy male ego to tell her that he had no trouble finding women, thank you very much. That this cabin was a voluntary retreat, not an involuntary sentence handed down from on high. But he didn't say that.

"What can I say? I've always had a weakness for Little Red Riding Hood."

She sighed, and at the end, it turned into a little laugh. "Very well. If that's what you want, I'll kiss you. But we leave for England as soon as possible."

"As you wish," Dominik murmured, everything in him hot and ready, laced through with triumph and something far darker and more intense he didn't want to name. Not when he could indulge it instead. "But first, that kiss. As promised."

CHAPTER FOUR

LAUREN WAS BAFFLED.

Why would anyone want a kiss—or, she supposed, a number of kisses—when there were so many other things he could have asked for? When the world was at his feet with the combined Combe and San Giacomo fortunes at his service?

She had met a great many men in her time, most of them through work, so she considered herself something of an expert in the behavior of males who considered themselves powerful. But she'd never met anyone like Dominik James. He had no power at all that she could see, but acted like he was the king of the world. It didn't make sense.

But it didn't matter. She wasn't here to understand the man. All she had to do was bring him back to London, and no matter that she felt a good deal less steady than she was pretending.

"Now?" she asked. She looked around the cabin as if sense was another rug tossed over the wood floor that could rise up and assert itself if she could only locate it. "You want me to kiss you *now*?"

Dominik lounged there before her, something glittering in the depths of his gray eyes, though the rest of his face was perfectly serious. He patted his knee with his free hand while what she thought was a smile *almost* changed the stern line of his mouth.

She pushed herself to her feet, still feeling that odd, liquid sensation all throughout her body. It was the way she felt when she slipped on a new pair of the shoes she loved. It made her feel...dangerous, almost. She'd always loved the feeling, because surely that was what a woman was meant to feel.

She'd long thought that if Matteo ever looked at her the way she looked at her shoes, she'd feel it. But he never had.

Lauren didn't understand why she felt it now, in a cabin in the middle of the woods. Or why Dominik was so determined to ruin it with more kissing.

Because the way he'd kissed her out there in the clearing had been different from her halfhearted youthful experiments, true. But Lauren knew it wouldn't last, because it never did. She knew that sooner or later he would grow ever more keen while she became less and less interested.

That was how it had always gone. She had discovered, time and again, that *thinking* about kissing was far preferable to the unfortunate reality of kissing.

She preferred this moment, right now. The moment when a man looked at her and imagined she was a desirable woman. Feminine straight through and capable of feeling all those things that real women did.

Capable of wanting and being wanted in return, when the truth was, *want* wasn't something that Lauren was capable of.

But he had already kissed her, and she told herself that was a good thing. She already knew what she'd agreed to. And it wasn't as if kissing Dominik had been as unpleasant as it always had been in the past.

Quite the opposite, a sly voice deep inside her very nearly purred.

She brushed that aside. It was the unexpected hike, no doubt, that had made her feel so flushed. So undone. She was unaccustomed to feeling those sorts of sensations in her body—all over her body—that was all.

"Perhaps you do not realize this, since you dislike kissing so much, but it is generally

not done while standing across the room,"
Dominik said with that thread of dark amusement woven into his voice that she couldn't
quite track. She could feel it, though. Deep
inside all those places where the hike through
the woods had made her sensitive.

She didn't understand that, either.

"Do you expect me to perch on your knee?"
she asked without trying all that hard to keep
the bafflement out of her voice.

"When and where I want," he said softly,
gray eyes alight. "How I want."

And Lauren was nothing if not efficient.
She had never been wanted, it was true, and
was lacking whatever that thing was that
could make her want someone else the way
others did so readily. So she had learned how
to be needed instead.

She had chosen to pursue a career as a personal assistant because there was no better
way to be needed—constantly—than to take
over the running of someone's life. She liked
the high stakes of the corporate world, but
what she loved was that Matteo truly *needed*
her. If she didn't do her job he couldn't do his.

He needed her to do this, too, she assured
herself. He wanted his brother in the fold,
media-ready and compliant, and she could
make it happen.

And if there was something inside her, some prickle of foreboding or something much sweeter and more dangerous, she ignored it.

The fire crackling beside them seemed hotter all of a sudden. It seemed to lick all over the side of her body, and wash across her face. She had never sat on a man's lap before, or had the slightest desire to do such a thing, and Dominik did nothing to help her along. He only watched her, no longer even the hint of a smile anywhere on his face, save the suggestion of one like silver in the endless gray of his gaze.

She stepped between his legs, thrust out before him in a way that encouraged her to marvel at both their length and strength, and then she eased herself down, putting out a hand to awkwardly prop herself against him as she sat.

"Do you plan to kiss me from this position?" She could swear he was laughing at her, though his face remained stern. "You are aware that kissing requires that lips meet, are you not?"

He had kissed her so smoothly out there at the edge of the woods. So easily. And now that Lauren thought about it, she had never been the one to initiate a kiss. She had always been a recipient. But there was something deep inside her that refused to tell him that.

It was the same something that bloomed with shame—because it had to be shame, surely—there between her legs.

She shouldn't have thought about that just then. Because she was sitting there on his hard, muscled thighs, so disastrously and intriguingly hot beneath her, and she couldn't seem to help herself from squirming against him.

And as she did she could feel something tense and electric hum to life in the space between them.

The fire was so hot. The air seemed to thicken with it as if there were flames dancing up and down the length of her arms, and the strangest part was that it didn't hurt. Burning should hurt, surely, but in this case it only seemed to make her breathless.

She eased closer to the wall of his chest, twisting herself so she was level with his face, and close enough to kiss him. Or she thought it was the correct distance, having never experimented with this position before.

He moved, but only a little, sliding his hands to grip her lightly at her waist.

Lauren couldn't think of a single reason why that should make her shudder.

Everywhere.

She gulped in a breath, aware of too many things at once. Those broad, blunt fingers of his like brands through the thin shell of her blouse. The iron forge of him beneath her, making her pulse and melt in places she'd never felt much of anything before.

This close, and knowing that a kiss was about to happen, she noticed things she hadn't before. The astonishing lines of his face, from his high cheekbones to the blade of his nose. The supremely male jut of his chin. And that thick, careless hair of his, that for some reason, she longed to sink her fingers into.

Her heartbeat slowed, but got louder. And harder, somehow, as if it was trying to escape from her chest.

She searched that implacable gray gaze of his, though she couldn't have said what she was looking for. She burned still, inside and out, and the fire seemed to come at her from all sides, not just from the fireplace.

Slowly, carefully, she lowered her mouth.

Then she pressed her lips against his.

For one long beat, there was only that. The trembling inside her, the feel of his firm lips beneath hers.

There, she thought, with a burst of satisfaction. *This is even easier than I expected—*

But that was when he angled his head.

And he didn't kiss the way she had, halting and unsure.

He smiled against her mouth, then licked his way inside, and Lauren...ignited.

It was as if the cabin caught fire and she was lost in the blaze.

She couldn't seem to get close enough. Dominik's big hands moved from her waist, snaking around her back to hold her even more fiercely. And she moved closer to him, letting her own hands go where they liked. His wide, hard shoulders. His deliciously scratchy jaw. And all that gloriously dark hair of his, thick and wild, like rough silk against her palms.

And still he kissed her, lazy and thorough at once, until she found herself meeting each thrust of his wicked tongue. Until she was the one angling her head, seeking that deliriously sweet fit.

As if they were interlocking parts, made of flame, intoxicating and dangerous at once.

Lauren was the one meant to be kissing him, and this was nothing but a bargain— but she forgot that. She forgot everything but the taste of him. His strength and all that fire, burning in her and around her until she thought she might have become her own blaze.

And she felt a different kind of need swell in her then, poignant and pointed all at once. It swept her from head to toe, then pooled in the place between her legs where she felt that fire most keenly and pulsed with a need too sharp to be shame—

She wrenched her lips from his, startled and shamed and something else that keened inside her, like grief.

For a moment there was nothing but that near-unbearable fire hanging in the air between them. His eyes were silver and bright, and locked to hers. That mouth of his was a temptation and a terror, and she didn't understand how any of this was happening.

She didn't understand much of anything, least of all herself.

"You promised," Lauren managed to say.

And would likely spend the rest of her life reliving how lost and small she sounded, and how little she thought she had it in her to fix it. Or fight her way back to her efficient and capable self.

"I did," he agreed.

His voice was a dark rasp that made her quiver all over again, deep inside.

"You promised and you've already broken that promise. It didn't even take you—"

Her voice cut off abruptly when he ran his

palm down the length of her ponytail and tugged it. Gently enough, so there was no reason she felt…scalded straight through.

"What promise did I break?" he asked mildly. So mildly she found herself frowning at him, because she didn't believe it.

"One kiss," she said severely.

And the way his mouth curved then, there below the knowing silver of his gaze, made her shiver.

"You're the one who has to say stop, little red. I don't remember you saying anything of the kind. Do you?"

And for another beat she was…stupefied.

Unable to breathe, much less react. Unable to do anything but gape at him.

Because he was quite right. She hadn't said anything at all.

In the next second she launched herself off him, leaping back in a way that she might have found comical, had she not been so desperate to put space between her and this man she'd made a devil's bargain with.

"This was our agreement, was it not?" Dominik asked, in that same mild voice. He only watched her—looking amused, she couldn't help but notice—as she scrambled around to the back of the chair facing him. "I hope you do not plan to tell me that you are already regretting the deal we made."

And Lauren did not believe in fairy tales. But it occurred to her, as she stared back at this man who had taken her over, made her a stranger to herself, and made her imagine that she could control something she very much feared was far more likely to burn her alive—she realized that she'd been thinking about the wrong kind of fairy tale.

Because there were the pretty ones, sweeping gowns and singing mice. Everything was princesses and musical numbers, neat and sweet and happy-ever-afters all around.

But those weren't the original fairy tales. There were darker ones. Older versions of the same stories, rich with the undercurrent of blood and sacrifice and grim consequences.

There were woods that swallowed you whole. Thorn bushes that stole a hundred years from your life. There were steep prices paid to devious witches, locked rooms that should have stayed closed, and children sent off to pay their fathers' debts in a variety of upsetting ways.

And there were men like Dominik, whose eyes gleamed with knowledge and certainty, and made her remember that there were some residents of hidden cottages who a wise girl never tried to find in the first place.

But Lauren hadn't heeded all the warnings. The man so difficult to find. The innkeeper's surprise that anyone would seek him out. That damned uninviting path through the woods.

She'd been so determined to prove her loyalty and capabilities to Matteo during this tough period in his life. If he wanted his long-lost older brother, she, by God, would deliver said older brother—once again making it clear that she alone could always, always give her boss what he needed.

Because she did so like to be needed.

She understood that then, with a lurch deep inside her, that once Matteo had mentioned Dominik this had always been where she would end up. This had always been her destination, which she had raced headlong toward with no sense of self-preservation at all.

This deal she'd made. And what it would do to her.

And she knew, with that same lurch and a kind of spinning sensation that threatened to take her knees out from under her, that it was already much too late to save herself from this thing she'd set in motion.

"I don't regret anything," she lied through

lips that no longer felt like hers. And though it was hard to meet that too-bright, too-knowing gray gaze of his, she forced herself to do it. And to hold it. "But we need to head back to England now. As agreed."

His lips didn't move, but she could see that smile of his, anyway. All wolf. All fangs.

As if he'd already taken his first bite.

"But of course," he said quietly. "I keep my promises, Lauren. Always. You would do well to remember that."

CHAPTER FIVE

BY THE TIME they made it down out of the mountains in the hardy SUV Dominik kept back behind the cabin, then onto the private plane Lauren had waiting for them at the nearest airfield, she'd convinced herself that she'd simply...gotten carried away.

Once out of the woods, the idea that she'd let *trees* get into her head and so deep beneath her skin struck her as the very height of foolishness.

She was a practical person, after all. She wasn't excitable. It was simply the combination of hiking around in heels and a man who considered kissing currency.

It was the oddness that had gotten to her, she told herself stoutly. And repeatedly.

By the time they boarded the plane, she had regained her composure. She was comfortable on the Combe Industries jet. In her element. She bustled into her usual seat, responded to her email and informed Matteo that she had not only found his brother, but would also shortly be delivering him to England. As requested.

It was amazing how completing a few basic tasks made her feel like herself again.

As if that strange creature who had lost herself on a strange man's lap had never existed at all.

She threw herself into the work that waited for her, delighted that it gave her the opportunity to continue pretending she had no idea who that girl could have been, wild with abandon on Dominik's knee. The farther they got from those woods, the farther she felt from all those bizarre sensations that had been stirred up in her.

Fairy tales, for God's sake. What had she been thinking?

Lauren resolved that she would do whatever she could to make sure she never succumbed to that kind of nonsense again, no matter what bargains she might have made to get Dominik on this plane.

But all through the short flight, no matter how ferociously she tried to concentrate on her computer screen and all the piled-up emails that required her immediate attention, she was aware of Dominik. Of that considering gray gaze of his, following her every move.

And worse, the heat it kicked up in its wake, winding around and around inside her until she was terribly afraid it would make her burst wide open.

Fairy tale nonsense, she told herself sharply. People didn't *burst,* no matter what they felt.

That was what came of tramping about in the wilderness. Too much clean air obviously made her take leave of her senses.

Back in London she felt even more like herself. Calm. Competent. In control and happily surrounded by tarmac. Concrete. Brick buildings. All the solid reminders of the world she knew. And preferred to inhabit, thank you very much.

"England's greenest hills appeared to be rather more gray puddles and a procession of dingy, squat holdings," Dominik said from beside her in the backseat of the car that picked them up from the private airfield outside the city. "What a disappointment."

Lauren congratulated herself on her total lack of reaction to him. He was nothing more than a business associate, sharing a ride.

"Surely, you must know that it rains in

England," she said, and even laughed. "A great deal, in fact."

She would have said nothing could possibly divert her attention from her mobile, but every cell in her body went on high alert when Dominik turned. And then faced her, making it impossible for her to pretend she didn't notice the way his big body took up more than his fair share of room in the car. His legs were too long, and those boots of his fascinated her. They seemed so utilitarian. So ruthlessly masculine.

And she couldn't even bring herself to think about the rest of him. All those long, smoothly muscled limbs. All that strength that simmered in him, that she was dimly surprised he managed to contain.

He didn't sit like a San Giacomo. He might look like one of them, or a feral version, anyway, but he was far more...elemental. Matteo and his sister, Pia, shared those same gray eyes, and they had both looked stormy at one time or another.

But Lauren couldn't help thinking that Dominik *was* a storm.

And her body reacted appropriately, prickling with unease—or maybe it was electricity.

Lightning, something in her whispered.

"What happens now?" Dominik asked, but his voice was lazy. Too lazy. She didn't believe he cared what happened now. Or ever. This was all a game to him.

Just as she was.

That thought flustered her, and she didn't make it any better by instantly berating herself for feeling anything at all. She tried to settle her nerves—the ones she didn't believe in—as she stared at him sternly.

"What would you like to happen?" she asked, and told herself she didn't know why she felt as if she were made of glass.

"I assume you are even now in the process of delivering me safely into the bosom of my warm, welcoming family." His smile was as sharp as she felt inside. Jagged. "Will there be a fatted calf?"

"I'm currently delivering you to the London headquarters of Combe Industries," Lauren replied as crisply as she could manage. Especially when all she could seem to concentrate on was his sardonic mouth. "Once there, you and I will wait for further instructions from Mr. Combe."

"Instructions." Dominik looked amused, if darkly. "I can hardly wait."

Lauren gripped her mobile in her hand and

made herself stop when she realized she was making her palm ache.

"Mr. Combe is actually not in England at present," she said, and she didn't know why she was telling him this now. It could have waited until they were out of this car. Until they were safely in the office, the place where she felt most at home. Most capable. "He is currently in Perth, Australia. He's personally visiting each and every Combe Industries office."

If Lauren had expected Matteo to greet the news that she'd found his brother by leaping onto a plane and heading straight home to meet him, she kept that to herself. Because Matteo showed no sign of doing anything of the kind.

And it felt disloyal to find that frustrating, but she did.

"The great saint is not in England?" Dominik asked in mock outrage. "But however will we know how best to serve him if he isn't here to lay out his wishes?"

"He is perfectly able to communicate his wishes at all times," she assured him. "It's actually my job to make certain he can, no matter where he is. Don't worry. You'll know exactly what he expects of you."

That was the wrong thing to say, but she

only realized that once the words were out there between them. And Dominik's eyes gleamed like silver as he gazed at her.

"Between you and me, little red, I have never done well with expectations." His voice was much too low for her peace of mind. It was too intimate. Too...insinuating. "I prefer to blaze my own trail."

"There is no blazing of trails in the San Giacomo family," she retorted with far more fervor than she'd intended. But she tried to keep her expression impassive when his dark brows rose. "The San Giacomos have existed in some form or another for centuries. They were once a major economic force in the Venetian Empire. While their economic force might have faded over time, their social capital has not."

"They sound marvelous," Dominik murmured. "And wholly without the blood of innocents on their hands, I am sure."

"I couldn't say what the San Giacomo family did in the eighth century, of course. But I think you'll find that Matteo Combe is a good and decent man."

"And you his greatest defender," Dominik said, and there was something less lazy about his voice then. "He must pay you very well indeed."

Her breath caught, but Lauren pushed on. "Whether you like expectations or do not, I'm afraid that the blood in your veins means you must meet them, anyway."

That dark amusement in Dominik's eyes made them bright against the rain outside. "Must I?"

"There are more eyes on the San Giacomos now than usual," Lauren said, and wasn't nervous. Why would she be nervous?

"It would seem to me that those eyes are more focused on the Combe side of the family," Dominik said after a moment. "Less Venetian economic might and more Yorkshire brawler, if I remember correctly."

Lauren didn't instantly bristle at that, which struck her as evidence of more disloyalty on her part.

"I'm not sure that there's any particular model of behavior for how a man is expected to act at his father's funeral," she said quietly. "Especially when his mother died only weeks before."

"I wouldn't know," Dominik replied, and that voice of his wasn't the least bit lazy any longer. "Having never met anyone who would claim me as a son in the first place."

Lauren felt as if he'd slapped her. Worse,

she felt a flush of shame as if she deserved the slap he hadn't actually given her.

"Why don't we wait to have this argument—"

Dominik laughed. "Is this an argument? You have a thin skin indeed, little red. I would have called this a discussion. And a friendly one, at that."

"—until we are in the office, and can bring Mr. Combe in on a call. Then he can answer all these questions instead of me, which seems more appropriate all around."

"Wonderful," Dominik said, and then his mouth curved in a manner she could only call challenging. "Kiss me."

And she had truly convinced herself that the bargain they'd struck had been some kind of hiking-inspired dream. A Hungarian-woods-inspired nightmare, made of altitude and too much wildlife. She had been sure it had all been some kind of hallucination. She'd been *sure.*

You're such a liar, a voice deep inside her told her.

"You can't mean now. Here."

"Will you make me say it every time?" Dominik's voice was soft, but the look on his face was intense. Intent. "When, where and how I want. Come now, Lauren. Are you a woman of your word or not?"

And it was worse, here. In the back of a town car like so many other town cars she'd ridden in, on this very same stretch of motorway. Here in England, on the outskirts of London, where she had always prided herself on her professionalism. Her competence and efficiency. Where she had built a life made entirely of needs she could meet, and did.

She still hadn't figured out who the Lauren Isadora Clarke was who had kissed this man with such abandon and hunger. But the intrusion of the fairy tale story she refused to accept was real into her life—her real life—was a shock. A jolt.

Her stomach went into free fall.

And Dominik shook his head sadly, making that *tsk*-ing sound as if he could read her every thought right there on her face. "You agreed to this bargain, Lauren. There's no use pretending you suddenly find the notion disgusting." His eyes were much too bright. "It is almost as if kissing makes you feel things, after all."

That shook her out of the grip of her horror—because that was what she told herself it had to be, that wild, spinning sensation that made her feel drunk from the inside out. It spurred her into action, and she didn't stop to question why it was she was so determined that this man never know that his kiss was the only one that had ever gotten to her at all.

It was information he never, ever needed to know.

She hardly wanted to admit it to herself.

And she threw herself across the backseat, determined that whatever else happened, she would do what she'd promised she would. That way, he would never know that she didn't want to do it *because* she wasn't bored by him the way she wanted to be.

Dominik caught her as she catapulted herself against his chest, then shifted her around so that she was sitting draped over his lap, which didn't help anything at all.

He was much too hard. There was the thick, enticing steel of his thighs, and that hard ridge that rose between them. And Lauren felt…soft and silly, and molten straight through.

And she was sitting on him again, caught in the way he gazed at her, silver in his eyes and his hands at her waist again.

"I know you know how to do this, little red," he said, his voice a soft taunt. "Or are you trying to play games with me?"

"I don't play games," she said stiffly.

As if, should she maintain proper posture

and a chilly tone, she might turn this impossible situation to her advantage. Or at least not drown in it.

"So many things you don't do," Dominik murmured, dark and sardonic. "Until you do."

She wanted him to stop talking. And she wanted to get this over with, as quickly as possible, and somehow those two things fused together and made it seem a terrific idea to lift her hands and use them to frame his face.

He stopped talking.

But the trouble with that was, her brain also stopped working.

She was entranced, suddenly and completely, with that strong jaw of his. She marveled at the feel of him, the rasp of his unshaven jaw beneath her palms.

A giant, hot fist she hadn't known lurked there inside her opened then. Slowly, surely, each finger of pure sensation unfurled, sending ribbons of heat to every last part of her.

She studied the sweep of his cheekbones, the lush shape of his mouth, and felt the shiver of it, so deep inside her it made parts she hadn't known she had bloom into life.

And she had the craziest urge to just...rub herself against him.

But instead, she kissed him.

She had some half-baked notion that she would deliver a peck, then retreat, but the moment she tasted him again she forgot about that. His mouth was a temptation and sin at once, and she was giddy with it. With his taste and heat.

With him, full stop.

So she angled her head and took the kiss deeper.

Just the way he'd taught her.

And for a little while, there was nothing at all but the slide of her tongue against his. The tangle of their breath, there in the close confines of the back of the car as it moved through the London streets.

Nothing but that humming thing that kicked up between them, encircling them both, then shuddering through Lauren until she worried, in some distant part of her head, that she would never be the same.

That she was already forever changed.

She kissed him and kissed him, and when she pulled her mouth away from his she fully expected him to follow her.

But he didn't.

She couldn't begin to describe the expression on his face then, or the steady sort of gleam in his gaze as he reached over and traced the shape of her mouth.

"Good girl," he said, and she knew without having to ask that he was deliberately trying to be provocative. "It's nice to know that you can keep your promise even after you get what you want."

"I am a woman of my word, Mr. James," she said crisply, remembering herself as she did.

And suddenly the fact that she was sitting on him, aware of all those parts of him pressed so intimately against her, was unbearable.

She scrambled off him and had the sinking suspicion that he let her go. And then watched her as if he could see straight through her.

And that was the thing. She believed he could.

It was unacceptable.

"The only thing you need to concern yourself about is the fact that you will soon be meeting your family for the first time," she said, frowning at him. "It wouldn't be surprising if you had some feelings around that."

"I have no feelings at all about that."

"I understand you may wish——"

"You do not understand." His voice was not harsh, but that somehow made the steel in it more apparent. "I was raised in an orphanage, Lauren. As an orphan. That means

I was told my parents were dead. When I was older, I learned that they might very well be alive, but they didn't want me, which I believed, given no one ever came to find me. I don't know what tearful, emotional reunion you anticipate I'm about to have with these people."

Lauren was horrified by the part of her that wanted to reach over to him again. This time, just to touch him. It was one more thing that didn't make sense.

"You're right, I can't understand. But I do know that Mr. Combe will do everything in his power to make sure this transition is easy for you."

"You are remarkably sure of your Mr. Combe. And his every thought."

"I've worked for him for a long time."

"With such devotion. And what exactly has he done to deserve your undying support?"

She flexed her toes in her shoes, and she couldn't have said why that made her feel so obvious, suddenly. Silly straight through, because he was looking at her. As if he could see every last thing about her, laid out on a plate before him.

Lauren didn't want to be known like that. The very notion was something like terrifying.

"I see," Dominik said, and there was a different sort of darkness in his voice then. "You are not sexual, you tell me with great confidence, but you are in love with your boss. How does that work, exactly?"

"I'm not in…" She couldn't finish the sentence, so horrified was she. "And I would never…" She wanted to roll down the window, let the cool air in and find her breath again, but she couldn't seem to move. Her limbs weren't obeying her commands. "Matteo Combe is one of the finest men I have ever known. I enjoy working for him, that's all."

She would never have said that she was in love with him. And she would certainly never have thought about him in any kind of sexual way. That seemed like a violation of all the years they'd worked together.

All she wanted—all she'd ever wanted—was for him to appreciate her. As a woman. To see her as something more than his walking, talking calendar.

"And this paragon of a man cannot stir himself to return home to meet the brother you claim he is so dedicated to? Perhaps, Lauren, you do not know the man you love so much as well as you think."

"I know him as well as I need to."

"And I know he's never tasted you," Dominik said with all his dark ruthlessness.

It made her want to cry. It made her want to... *do something* with all that restlessness inside her. "Has he?"

Lauren could barely breathe. Her cheeks were so red she was sure they could light up the whole of the city on their own.

"Not answering the question is an answer all its own, little red," Dominik murmured, his face alight with what she very much feared was satisfaction.

And she was delighted—relieved beyond measure—that the car pulled up in front of the Combe Industries building before she was forced to come up with some kind of reply.

But she didn't pretend it was anything but a reprieve, and likely a temporary one, when she pushed open the door and threw herself out into the blessedly cool British evening.

Where she tried—and failed, again and again—to catch her breath and recover from the storm that was Dominik James.

CHAPTER SIX

THERE WAS NO doubt at all that the man on the video screen was Dominik's brother. It was obvious from the shape of his jaw to the gray of his eyes. His hair was shorter, and every detail about him proclaimed his wealth and high opinion of himself. The watch he wore that he wasn't even bothering to try to flash. The cut of his suit. The way he sat as if the mere presence of his posterior made wherever he rested it a throne.

This was the first blood relative Dominik had ever met, assuming a screen counted as a meeting. This…aristocrat.

He couldn't think of a creature more diametrically opposed to him. He, who had suffered and fought for every scrap he'd ever had, and a man who looked as if he'd never blinked without the full support of a trained staff.

They stared at each other for what seemed like another lifetime or two.

Dominik stood in Lauren's office, which was sprawling and modern and furnished in such a way to make certain everyone who entered it knew that she was very important in her own right—and even more so, presumably, as the gatekeeper to the even more massive and dramatically appointed office beyond.

Matteo Combe's office, Dominik did not have to be told.

His only brother, so far as he knew. The man who had received all the benefit of the blood they shared, while Dominik had been accorded all the shame.

Matteo Combe, the man whose bidding Lauren did without question.

Dominik decided he disliked the man on the screen before him. Intensely.

"I would have known you anywhere," Matteo said after they'd eyed each other a good long while.

It would have pained Dominik to admit that he would have known Matteo, too—it was the eyes they shared, first and foremost, and a certain similarity in the way they held themselves—so he chose not to admit it.

"Brother," Dominik replied instead, practically drawling out the word. Making it something closer to an insult. "What a pleasure to almost meet you."

And when Lauren showed him out of the office shortly after that tender reunion, Dominik took a seat in the waiting area that was done up like the nicest and most expensive doctor's office he'd ever seen, and reflected on how little he'd thought about this part. The actually having family, suddenly, part.

Because all he'd thought about since she'd walked into his clearing was Lauren.

When he'd searched for his parents, he'd quickly discovered that the young man who'd had the temerity to impregnate an heiress so far above his own station had died in an offshore oil rig accident when he was barely twenty. An oil rig he'd gone to work on because he couldn't remain in Europe, pursuing his studies, after his relationship with Alexandrina had been discovered.

And when Dominik had found all the Combes and San Giacomos with precious little effort—which, of course, meant they could have done the same—he'd had wanted nothing to do with them. Because he wanted nothing from them—look what they'd done to the boy who'd fathered him. They had gotten rid of both of them, in one way or another, and Dominik had risen from the trash heap where they'd discarded him despite that abandonment. His mother's new boy and girl, who had been pampered and coddled and cooed over all this time in his stead, were nothing to him. What was the point of meeting with them to discuss Alexandrina's sins?

He'd been perfectly content to excel on his own terms, without any connection to the great families who could have helped him out of the gutter, but hadn't. Likely because they'd been the ones to put him there.

But it hadn't occurred to him to prepare himself to look into another man's face and see…his own.

It was disconcerting, to put it mildly.

That they had different fathers was evident, but there was no getting around the fact that he and Matteo Combe shared blood. Dominik scowled at the notion, because it sat heavily. Too heavily.

And then he transferred that scowl back to the screen inside Lauren's office, where Matteo was still larger than life and Lauren stood before him, arguing.

He didn't have to be able to hear a word she said to know she was arguing. He knew some of her secrets now. He knew the different shapes she made with that mouth of hers and the crease between her brows that broadcast her irritation. He certainly knew what she looked like when she was agitated.

And he found he didn't much care for the notion that whatever she called it or didn't call it, she had a thing for her boss.

Her boss. His brother.

"Is he one of the ones you've experimented with?" he asked her when she came out of the office, the screen finally blank behind her.

She was frowning even more fiercely than before, which he really shouldn't have found entertaining, especially when he hadn't had the pleasure of causing it. He lounged back in his seat as if it had been crafted specifically for him and regarded her steadily until she blinked. In what looked like incomprehension.

"I already declined to dignify that question with a response."

"Because dignity is the foremost concern here. With your boss." He refused to call the man *Mr. Combe* the way she did. And calling him by his Christian name seemed to suggest that they had more of a personal relationship—or any personal relationship, for that matter—than Dominik was comfortable having with anyone who shared his blood. "I want to know if he was one of your kissing experiments."

Lauren maintained her blank expression for a moment.

But then, to his eternal delight, she went pink and he couldn't seem to keep from wondering about all the other, more exciting ways he could make her flush like that.

"Certainly not." Her voice was frigid, but he'd tasted her. He knew the ice she tried to hide behind was a lie. "I told you, I admire him. I enjoy the work we do together. I have never *kissed*—"

She cut herself off, then pulled herself up straight. It only made Dominik wonder what she might have said if she hadn't stopped herself. "You and I have far more serious things to talk about than kissing experiments, Mr. James."

"I have always found kissing very serious business indeed. Would you like me to demonstrate?"

That pink flush deepened and he wanted to know where it went. If it changed as it lowered to her breasts, and what color her nipples were. If it made it to her hips, her thighs. And all that sweetness in between. He wanted to peel off that soft silk blouse she wore and conduct his own experiments, at length.

And the fact that thinking about Lauren Clarke's naked body was far preferable to him than considering the fact he'd met his brother, more or less, did not escape him. Dominik rarely hid from himself.

But he had no need, and less desire, to tear himself open and seek out the lonely orphan inside.

"Mr. Combe thinks it best that we head to Combe Manor. It is the estate in Yorkshire where his father's family rose to prominence. He understands you are not a Combe. But he thinks it would cause more comment to bring you directly to any of the San Giacomo holdings in Italy at this point."

Dominik understood that *at this point* was the most important part of Lauren's little speech. That and the way she delivered it, still standing in her own doorway too stiffly, her voice a little too close to nervous. He studied her and watched her grow even more agitated—and then try to hide it.

It was the fact that she wanted to hide her reactions from him that made him happiest of all, he thought.

"I don't know who you think is paying such close attention to me," Dominik said after a moment. "No one has noticed that I bear more than a passing resemblance to a member of the San Giacomo family in my entire lifetime so far. I cannot imagine that will change all of a sudden."

"It will change in an instant should you be found in a San Giacomo residence, looking as you do, as the very ghost of San Giacomos past."

He inclined his head. Slightly. "I am very good at living my life away from prying eyes, little red. You may have noticed."

"Those days are over now." She stood even straighter, and he had the distinct impression she was working herself up to say something else. "You may not feel any sense of urgency, but I can tell you that the clock is ticking. It's only a matter of time before Alexandrina's will is leaked, because these things are always leaked. Once it is, the paparazzi will tear apart the earth to find you. We need to be prepared for when that happens."

"I feel more than prepared already. In the sense of not caring."

"There are a number of things it would make more sense for us to do now, before the world gets its teeth into you."

"How kinky," he murmured, just to please himself.

And better still, to make her caramel eyes

flash with that temper he suspected was the most honest thing about her.

"First, we must make your exterior match the San Giacomo blood that runs in your veins."

He found his mouth curving. "Are you suggesting a makeover? Have I strayed into a fairy tale, after all?"

"I certainly wouldn't call it that. A bit of tailoring and a new wardrobe, that's all. Perhaps a lesson or two in minor comportment issues that might arise. And a haircut, definitely."

Dominik's grin was sharp and hot. "Why, Lauren. Be still my heart. Am I the Cinderella in this scenario? I believe that makes you my Princess Charming."

"There's no such thing as a Princess Charming." She sniffed. "And anyway, I believe my role here is really as more of a Fairy Godmother."

"I do not recall Cinderella and her Fairy Godmother ever being attached at the lips," he said silkily. "But perhaps your fairy tales are more exciting than mine ever were."

"I hate fairy tales," she threw at him. "They're strange little stories designed to make children meek and biddable and responsible for the things that happen to them when they're not. And also, we need to get married."

That sat there between them, loud and not a little mad.

Dominik's gaze was fused to hers and, sure enough, that flush was deepening. Darkening.

"I beg your pardon." He lingered over each word, almost as if he really was begging. Not that he had any experience with such things. And there was so much to focus on, but he had to choose. "All this urban commotion must be getting to me." He made a show of looking all around the empty office, then, because he had never been without a flair for the dramatic when it suited him—and this woman brought it out in him in spades. "Did you just ask me to marry you?"

"I'm not *asking* you, personally. I'm telling you that Mr. Combe thinks it's the best course of action. First, it will stop the inevitable flood of fortune hunters who will come out of the woodwork once they know you exist before they think to start. Second, it will instantly make you seem more approachable and civilized, because the world thinks married men are less dangerous, somehow, than unattached ones. Third, and most important, it needn't be real in any sense but the boring legalities. And we will divorce as soon as the furor settles."

Dominik only gazed back at her, still and watchful.

"Come now, Lauren. A man likes a little romance, not a bullet-pointed list. The very least you could do is bend a knee and mouth a sweet nothing or two."

"I'm not *proposing* to you!" Her veneer slipped at that, and her face reddened. "Mr. Combe thinks—"

"Will I be marrying my own brother?" He lay his hand over his heart in mock astonishment. "What sort of family *is* this?"

He thought her head might explode. He watched her hands curl into fists at her sides as if that alone could keep her together.

"You agreed to do whatever was asked of you," she reminded him, fiercely. "Don't tell me that you're the one who's going to break our deal. Now. After—"

After kissing him repeatedly, he knew she meant to say, but she stopped herself.

The more he stared back at her without saying a word, the more agitated she became. And the more he enjoyed himself, though perhaps that made him a worse man than even he'd imagined. And he'd spent a great quantity of time facing his less savory attributes head-on, thanks in part to the ministrations of the nuns who had taught him shame and how best to hate himself for existing. The army had taken care of the rest.

These days Dominik was merrily conversant on all his weaknesses, but Lauren made him…something else again.

But that was one more thing he didn't want to focus on.

"What would be the point of a marriage that wasn't real?" he asked idly. "The public will need to have reason to believe it's real for it to be worth bothering, no?"

The truth was that Dominik had never thought much about marriage one way or the other. Traditional family relationships weren't something he had ever seen modeled in the orphanage or on the streets in Spain. He had no particular feelings about the state of marriage in any personal sense, except that he found it a mystifying custom, this strange notion that two people should share their lives. Worse, themselves.

And odder still, call it love—of all things—while they did it.

What Dominik knew of love was what the nuns had doled out in such a miserly way, always shot through with disappointment, too many novenas and demands for better behavior. Love was indistinguishable from its unpleasant consequences and character assassinations, and Dominik had been much happier when he'd left all that mess and failure behind him.

He had grown used to thinking of himself as a solitary being, alone by choice rather than circumstance. He liked his own company. He was content to avoid others. And he enjoyed the peace and quiet that conducting his affairs to his own specifications, with no outside opinion and according to his own wishes and whims, afforded him. He was answerable to no one and chained to nothing.

The very notion of marrying anyone, for any reason, should have appalled him.

But it didn't.

Not while he gazed at this woman before him—

That pricked at him, certainly. But not enough to stop. Or leave, the way he should have already.

He told himself it was because this was a game, that was all. An amusement. What did he care about the San Giacomo reputation or public opinion? He didn't.

But he did like the way Lauren Clarke tasted when she melted against him. And it appeared he liked toying with her in between those meltings, too.

"What we're talking about is a publicity stunt, nothing more," she told him, frowning all the while. "You understand what that means, don't you? There's nothing real about it. It's entirely temporary. And when it ends, we will go our separate ways and pretend it never happened."

"You look distressed, little red," he murmured, because all she seemed to do as she stood there before him was grow redder and stiffer, and far more nervous, if the way she wrung her hands together was any indication.

He didn't think she had the slightest idea what she was doing. Which was fair enough, as neither did he. Evidently. Since he was still sitting here, lounging about in the sort of stuffy corporate office he'd sworn off when he'd sold his company, as if he was obedient. When he was not. Actually subjecting himself to this charade.

Participating in it wholeheartedly, in point of fact, or he never would have invited her into his cabin. Much less left it in her company— then flown off to rainy, miserable England.

"I wouldn't call myself distressed." But her voice told him otherwise. "I don't generally find business concerns *distressing*. Occasionally challenging, certainly."

"And yet I am somehow unconvinced." He studied the way she stood. The way she bit at her lower lip. Those hands that telegraphed the feelings she claimed not to have. "Could it be that your Mr. Combe, that paragon of virtue and all that is wise and true in an employer by your reckoning, has finally pushed you too far?"

"Of course not." She seemed to notice what she was doing with her hands then, because she dropped them back to her sides. Then she drew herself up in that way she did, lifted her chin and met his gaze. With squared shoulders and full-on challenge in her caramel-colored eyes—which, really, he shouldn't have found quite as entertaining as he did. What was it about this woman? Why did he find her so difficult to resist? He, who had made a life out of resisting everything? "Perhaps you've already forgotten, but you promised that you would do whatever was asked of you."

He stopped trying to control his grin. "I recall my promises perfectly, thank you. I am shocked and appalled that you think so little of the institution of marriage that you would suggest wedding me in some kind of cold-blooded attempt to fool the general populace, all of whom you appear to imagine will be hanging on our every move."

He shook his head at her as if disappointed unto his very soul at what she had revealed here, and had the distinct pleasure of watching her grit her teeth.

"I find it difficult to believe that you care one way or the other," she said after a moment. "About fooling anyone for any reason. And, for that matter, about marriage."

"I don't." He tilted his head to one side. "But I suspect you do."

He thought he'd scored a hit. She stiffened further, then relaxed again in the next instant as if determined not to let him see it. And then her cheeks flamed with that telltale color, which assured him that yes, she cared.

But a better question was, why did he?

"I don't have any feelings about marriage at all," she declared in ringing tones he couldn't quite bring himself to believe. "It was never something I aspired to, personally, but I'm not opposed to it. I rarely think about it at all, to be honest. Are you telling me that you lie awake at night, consumed with fantasies about your own wedding, Mr. James?"

"Naturally," he replied. And would have to examine, at some point, why he enjoyed pretending to be someone completely other than who he was where this woman was concerned. Purely for the pleasure of getting under her skin. He smiled blandly. "Who among us has not dreamed of swanning down an expensive aisle, festooned in tulle and lace, for the entertainment of vague acquaintances?"

"Me," she retorted at once. And with something like triumph in her voice.

"Of course not, because you are devoid of feelings entirely, as you have taken such pains to remind me."

"I'm not sentimental." Except she looked so deeply pleased with herself just then it looked a whole lot like an emotion, whether she wanted to admit such things or not. "I apologize if you find that difficult to accept."

"You have no feelings about marriage. Sex. Even kissing, no matter how you react while doing it. You're an empty void, capable only of doing the bidding of your chosen master. I understand completely, Lauren."

That she didn't like that description was obvious by the way she narrowed her eyes, and the way she flattened her lips. Dominik smiled wider. Blander.

"How lucky your Mr. Combe is to have found such devotion, divorced of any inconvenient sentiment on your part. You might as well be a robot, cobbled together from spare parts for the singular purpose of serving his needs."

If her glare could have actually reached across the space between them and struck him then, Dominik was sure he would have sustained mortal blows. What he was less certain of was why everything in him objected to thinking of her as another man's. In any capacity.

"What I remember of my parents' marriage is best not discussed in polite company," she said, her voice tight. He wondered if she knew how the sound betrayed her. How it broadcast the very feelings she pretended not to possess. "They divorced when I was seven. And they were both remarried within the year, which I didn't understand until later meant that they had already moved on long before the ink was dry on their divorce decree. The truth is that they only stayed as long as they did because neither one wanted to take responsibility for me." She shook her head, but more as if she was shaking something off than negating it. "Believe me, I know better than anyone that most marriages are nothing but a sham. No matter how much tulle and expense there might be. That doesn't make me a robot. It makes me realistic."

Something in the way she said that clawed at him, though he couldn't have said why. Or didn't want to know why, more accurately, and accordingly shoved it aside.

"Wonderful," he said instead. "Then you will enjoy our sham of a marriage all the more, in all its shabby realism."

"Does that mean you'll do it, then?"

And he didn't understand why he wanted so badly to erase that brittleness in her tone. Why he wanted to reach out and touch her in ways that had nothing to do with the fire in him, but everything to do with that hint of vulnerability he doubted she knew was so visible. In the stark softness of her mouth. In the shadows in her eyes.

"I will do it," he heard himself say. "For you."

And every alarm he'd ever wired there inside him screeched an alert then, at full volume.

Because Dominik did not do things for other people. No one was close enough to him to ask for or expect that kind of favor. No one got close to him. And in return for what he'd always considered peace, he kept himself at a distance from everyone else. No obligations. No expectations.

But there was something about Lauren, and how hard she was clearly fighting to look unfazed in the face of her boss's latest outrageous suggestion. As if an order to marry the man's unknown half brother was at all reasonable.

You just agreed to it, a voice in him pointed out. *So does it matter if it's reasonable?*

One moment dragged on into another, and then it was too late to take the words back. To qualify his acceptance. To make it clear that no matter what he might have said, he hadn't meant it to stand as any form of obligation to this woman he barely knew.

Much less that boss of hers who shared his blood.

"For me?" she asked, and it was as if she, too, had suddenly tumbled into this strange, hushed space Dominik couldn't seem to snap out of.

He didn't want to call it sacred. But he wasn't sure what other word there was for it, when her caramel eyes gleamed like gold and his chest felt tight.

"For you," he said, and he had the sense that he was digging his own grave, shovelful by shovelful, whether he wanted it or not. But even that didn't stop him. He settled farther back against his chair, thrust his legs out another lazy inch and let one corner of his mouth crook. "But if you want me to marry you, little red, I'm afraid I will require a full, romantic proposal."

She blinked. Then swallowed.

"You can't be serious."

"I don't intend to make a habit of marrying. This will have to be perfect, the better to live on all my days." He nodded toward the polished wood at his feet. "Go on, then. On your knees, please."

And he was only a man. Not a very good one, as he'd acknowledged earlier. There was no possibility of issuing such an order without imagining all the other things she could do once she was there.

So he did. And had to shift slightly where he sat to accommodate the hungriest part of him.

"You agreed that any marriage between us will be a sham," she was saying, her voice a touch too husky for someone so dedicated to appearing unmoved. "You used that very word. It will be a publicity stunt, and only a publicity stunt, as I said."

"Whatever the marriage is or isn't, it begins right here." He ignored the demands that clamored inside him, greedy and still drunk on his last taste of her. "Where there is no public. No paparazzi. No overbearing employer who cannot stir himself to greet his long-lost brother in person."

She started to argue that but subsided when he shook his head.

"There are only two people who ever need to know how this marriage began, Lauren. And we are both right here, all alone, tucked away on an abandoned office floor where no one need ever be the wiser."

She rolled her eyes. "We can tell them there was kneeling all around, if that's really what you need."

"We can tell them anything you like, but I want to see a little effort. A little care, here between the two of us. A pretty, heartfelt proposal. Come now, Lauren." And he smiled at her then, daring her. "A man likes to be seduced."

Her cheeks had gone pale while he spoke, and as he watched, they flooded with bright new color.

"You don't want to be seduced. You want to humiliate me."

"Six of one, half dozen of another." He jutted his chin toward the floor again. "You need to demonstrate your commitment. Or how else will I know that my heart is safe in your hands?"

The color on her cheeks darkened, and her eyes flashed with temper. And he liked that a hell of a lot more than her robot impression.

"No one is talking about hearts, Mr. James," she snapped at him. "We're talking about damage control. Optics. PR."

"You and your Mr. Combe may be talking about all of those things," he said and shrugged. "But I am merely a hermit from a Hungarian hovel, too long-haired to make sense of your complicated corporate world. What do I know of such things? I'm a simple man, with simple needs." He reached up and dramatically clasped his chest, never shifting his gaze from hers. "If you want me, you must convince me. On your knees, little red."

She made a noise of sheer, undiluted frustration that nearly made him laugh. Especially when it seemed to make her face that much brighter.

He watched as she forced her knees to unlock. She took a breath in, then let it out. Slowly, as if it hurt, she took a step toward him. Then another.

And by the time she moved past his feet, then insinuated herself right where he wanted her, there between his outstretched legs, he didn't have the slightest urge to laugh any longer. Much less when she sank down on her knees before him, just as he'd imagined in all that glorious detail.

She knelt as prettily as she did everything else, and she filled his head as surely as his favorite Hungarian *palinka*. He couldn't seem to look away from her, gold and pink and that wide caramel gaze, peering up at him from between his own legs.

The sight of her very nearly unmanned him.

And he would never know, later, how he managed to keep his hands to himself.

"Dominik James," she said softly, looking up at him with eyes wide, filled with all those emotions she claimed she didn't feel— but he did, as if she was tossing them straight into the deepest part of him, "will you do me the honor of becoming my husband? For a while?"

He didn't understand why something in him kicked against that qualification. But he ignored it.

He indulged himself by reaching forward and fitting his palm to the curve of her cheek. He waited until her lips parted because he knew she felt it, too, that same heat that roared in him. That wildfire that was eating him alive.

"But of course," he said, and he had meant

to sound sardonic. Darkly amused. But that wasn't how it came out, and he couldn't think of a way to stop it. "I can think of nothing I would like to do more than marry a woman I hardly know to serve the needs of a brother I have never met in the flesh, to save the reputation of a family that tossed me aside like so much trash."

There was a sheen in her gaze that he wanted to believe was connected to that strangely serious thing in him, not laughing at all. And the way her lips trembled, just slightly.

Just enough to make the taste of her haunt him all over again.

"I... I can't tell if that's a yes or no."

"It's a yes, little red," he said, though there was no earthly reason that he should agree to any of this.

There was no reason that he should even be here, so far away from the life he'd carved out to his specifications. The life he had fought so hard to win for himself.

But Lauren had walked into his cabin, fit too neatly into the chair that shouldn't have been sitting there, waiting for her, and now he couldn't seem to keep himself from finding out if she fit everywhere else, too.

A thought that was so antithetical to everything he was and everything he believed to be true about himself that Dominik wasn't sure why he didn't trust her away from him and leave. Right now.

But he didn't.

Worse, he didn't want to.

"It's a yes," he said, his voice grave as he betrayed himself, and for no reason, "but I'm afraid, as in most things, there will be a price. And you will be the one to pay it."

CHAPTER SEVEN

Lauren didn't understand anything that was happening.

She had been astounded when Matteo had suggested marriage, so offhandedly as if it was perfectly normal to run around marrying strangers on a whim because he thought that would look better in some theoretical tabloid.

"Marry him," he'd said, so casually, from the far side of the world. "You are a decent, hardworking sort and you've been connected to the family without incident for years."

"I think you mean employed by the family and therefore professional."

"You can take him in hand. Make sure he's up to the task. And by the time the shock fades over my mother's scandalous past, you'll have made him everything he needs to be to take his place as a San Giacomo."

"Will this new role come with combat pay?" she'd asked, with more heat than she normally used with her boss, no matter what was going on. But then, she wasn't normally dispatched into the hinterland, made to *hike*, and then kissed thoroughly and repeatedly. She was…not herself. "Or do you expect me to give up my actual life for the foreseeable future for my existing salary, no questions asked?"

She never spoke to Matteo that way. But he didn't normally react the way he had then, either, with nothing but silence and what looked very much like sadness on his face. It made Lauren wish she hadn't said anything.

Not for the first time, she wondered exactly what had gone on between Matteo and the anger management consultant the Combe Industries board of directors had hired in a transparent attempt to take Matteo down. He'd gone off with her to Yorkshire, been unusually unreachable and then had set off on a round-the-world tour of all the Combe Industries holdings.

A less charitable person might wonder if he was attempting to take the geographic tour.

"You can name your price, Lauren," he said after what felt like a very long while, fraught with all the evidence she'd ever needed that though they might work very closely together, they had no personal relationship. Not like that. "All I ask is that you tame this brother of mine before we unleash him on the world. The board will not be pleased to have more scandal attached to the Combe name. And the least we can do is placate them a little."

And she'd agreed to ask Dominik, because what else could she do? For all Dominik's snide commentary, the truth was that she admired Matteo. He was not his father, who had always been willing to take the low road— and usually had. Matteo had integrity, something she knew because no matter how she might have longed for him to *see* her, he never had. He treated her as his personal assistant, not as a woman. It was why she felt safe while she wore her outrageously feminine heels. It was why she felt perfectly happy dedicating herself to him.

If he had looked at her the way Dominik did, even once, she would never have been able to work for him at all. She would never have been able to sort out what was an appropriate request and what wasn't, and would have lost herself somewhere in the process.

She'd been reeling from that revelation when she'd walked out to pitch the marriage idea, fully expecting that Dominik would laugh at the very notion.

But he hadn't.

And she'd meant to present the whole thing as a very dry and dusty sort of business proposition, anyway. Just a different manner of merger, that was all. But instead of a board meeting of sorts, she was knelt down between his legs, gazing up at him from a position that made her whole body quiver.

And unless she was very much mistaken, he had actually agreed to marry her.

For a price.

Because with this man, there was always a price.

How lucky you want so badly to pay it, an insinuating, treacherous voice from deep inside her whispered. *Whatever it is.*

"What kind of price?" Lauren frowned at him as if that could make them both forget that she was kneeling before him like a supplicant. Or a lover. And that he was touching her as if at least one of those things was a foregone conclusion. "I have already promised to kiss you whenever you like. What more could you want?"

His palm was so hard and hot against the side of her face. She felt it everywhere, and she knew that seemingly easy touch was responsible for the flames she could feel licking at her. All over her skin, then deeper still, sweet and hot in her core.

Until she *throbbed* with it. With him.

"Do you think there are limits to what a man might want?" he asked quietly, and his voice was so low it set her to shattering, like a seismic event. Deep inside, where she was already molten and more than a little afraid that she might shake herself apart.

"You're talking about sex again," she said, and thought she sounded something like solemn. Or despairing. And neither helped with all that unbearable *heat*. "I don't know how many ways I can tell you—"

"That you are not sexual, yes, I am aware." He moved his thumb, dragging it gently across her lower lip, and his mouth crooked when she hissed in a breath. His eyes blazed when goose bumps rose along her neck and ran down her arms, and his voice was little more than a growl when he spoke again. "Not sexual at all."

Something in the way he said that made her frown harder, though she already knew it was futile. And it only seemed to make that terrible, knowing blaze in his gray eyes more pronounced.

And much, much hotter. Inside her, where she still couldn't tell if she hated it—or loved it.

"What do you want from me?" she asked, her voice barely above a whisper.

And she thought that whatever happened, she would always remember the way he smiled at her then, half wolf and all man. That it was tattooed inside her, branded into her flesh, forever a part of her. Whether she liked it or not.

"What I want from you, little red, is a wedding night."

That was another brand, another scar. And far more dangerous than before.

Lauren's throat was almost too dry to work. She wasn't sure it would. "You mean...?"

"I mean in the traditional sense, yes. With all that entails."

He shifted, and she had never felt smaller. In the sense of being delicate. *Precious*, something in her whispered, though she knew that was fanciful. And worse, foolish.

Dominik smoothed his free hand over her hair, and let it rest at the nape of her neck. And the way he held her face made something in her do more than melt.

She thought maybe it sobbed.

Or she did.

"Find a threshold, and I will carry you over it," he told her, his voice low and intent. And the look in his gray eyes so male, very nearly *possessive*, it made her ache. "I will lay you down on a bed and I will kiss you awhile, to see where it goes. And all I need from you is a promise that you will not tell me what you do and do not like until you try it. That's all, Lauren. What do you have to lose?"

And she couldn't have named the things she had to lose, because they were all the one thing—they were all *her*—and she was sure he would take them, anyway.

He would take everything.

Maybe she'd known that from the moment she'd seen the shadows become a man, there in that clearing so far from the rest of the world. There in those woods that had taunted her from the first, whispering of darkness and mystery in a thousand ways she hadn't wanted to hear.

Maybe it had always been leading straight here.

But between the heat of his hands and that shivering deep inside her, she couldn't seem to mind it as much as she should have.

As much as she suspected she would, once she survived this. *If* she survived this.

She should get up right this minute. She should move herself out of danger—out of arm's reach. She should tell Dominik she didn't care what he did with his newfound name and fortune, just as she should ring Matteo back and tell him she had no intention of marrying a stranger on command.

She knew she should do all those things. She *wanted* to do all those things.

But instead, she shivered. And in that moment, there at his feet with all his focus and intent settled on her, she surrendered.

If surrender was a cliff, Lauren leaped straight off it, out into nothing. She hadn't done anything so profoundly foolish since she was nine years old and had thought she could convince her parents to pay more attention to her by acting out. She'd earned herself instead an unpleasant summer in boarding school.

But surrendering here, to Dominik, didn't feel like that. It didn't feel like plummeting down into sharp rocks.

It felt far more like flying.

"I will give you a wedding night," she heard herself agree, her voice very stern and matter-of-fact, as if that could mask the fact that she was capitulating. As if she could divert his attention from the great cliff she'd just flung herself over. "But that's all."

"Perhaps we will leave these intimate negotiations until after the night in question," Dominik said, that undercurrent of laughter in his voice. "You may find you very much want a honeymoon, little red. Who knows? Perhaps even an extended one. This may come as a surprise to you, but there are some women who would clamor for the opportunity to while away some time in my bed."

Wedding nights. Honeymoons. *Time in bed.* This was all a farce. It had to be.

But Lauren was on her knees in the offices of Combe Industries, and she had just proposed marriage to a man she'd only met this morning.

So perhaps *farce* wasn't quite the right word to describe what was happening.

Something traitorous inside her wanted to lean in closer, and that terrified her, so she took it as an opportunity to pull away. Cliff or no cliff.

Except he didn't let her.

That hand at her nape held her fast, and something about that…lit her up. It was as if she didn't know what she was doing any longer. Or at all. But maybe he did.

And suddenly she was kneeling up higher, her hands flat on his thighs, her face tilted toward his in a manner she could have called all kinds of names.

All of them not the least bit her. Not the person she was or had ever been.

But maybe she was tired of Lauren Isadora Clarke. And everything she'd made herself become while she was so busy not feeling things.

Like this. Like him.

"It's not a real proposal until there's a kiss, Lauren," Dominik told her. Gruffly, she thought. "Even you must know this."

"Isn't it enough that I promised you a wedding night?" she asked, and she might have been horrified at the way her voice cracked at that, but there were so many horrors to sift through. Too many.

And all of them seemed to catch fire and burn brighter as she knelt there between his legs, not sure if she felt helpless or far more alarming, *alive*.

Alive straight through, which only made it clear that she never had been before. Not really.

"Kiss me, little red," he ordered her, almost idly. But there was no mistaking the command in his voice all the same. "Keep your promise."

His voice might have been soft, but it was ruthless. And his gray eyes were pitiless.

And he didn't seem to mind in the least when she scowled at him, because it was the only thing she knew how to do.

"Now, please," he murmured in that same demanding way. "Before you hurt my feelings."

She doubted very much that his feelings had anything to do with this, but she didn't say that. She didn't want to give him more opportunity to comment on hers. Or call her a robot again.

"I don't understand why you would want to kiss someone who doesn't wish to kiss you," she threw at him in desperation.

"I wouldn't." Those gray eyes laughed at her. "But that description doesn't apply to either one of us, does it?"

"One of us is under duress."

"One of us, Lauren, is a liar."

She could feel the heat that told her that her cheeks were red, and she had the terrible notion that meant he was right. And worse, that he could see it all over her face.

She had no idea.

In a panic, she mimicked him, hooking one hand around the hard column of his neck and pulling his mouth to hers.

This man who had agreed to marry her. To pretend, anyway, and there was no reason that should work in her the way it did, like a powder keg on the verge of exploding. Like need and loss and yearning, tangled all together in an angry knot inside her.

And she was almost used to this now. The delirious slide, the glorious fire, of their mouths together.

He let her kiss him, let her control the angle and the depth, and she made herself shiver as she licked her way into his mouth. All the while telling herself that she didn't like this. That she didn't want this.

And knowing with every drugging slide of his tongue against hers that he'd been right all along.

She was a liar.

Maybe that was why, when his hands moved to trace their way down her back, she moaned at the sensation instead of fighting it. And when he pulled her blouse from the waistband of her formal trousers, she only made a deeper noise, consumed with the glory of his mouth.

And the way he kissed her and kissed her, endless and intoxicating.

But then his bare hand was on her skin, moving around to the front of her and then finally—finally, as if she'd never wanted anything more when she'd never wanted it in the first place, when it had never occurred to her to imagine such a thing—closing over the swell of one breast.

And everything went white around the edges.

Her breast seemed to swell, filling his palm, with her nipple high and hard.

And every time he moved his palm, she felt it like another deep lick—

But this time in the hottest, wildest, most molten place of all between her legs.

She could feel his other hand in her hair, cradling the back of her head and holding her mouth where he wanted it, making absolutely no bones about the fact that he was in charge.

And it was thrilling.

Lauren arched her back, giving him more of her, and it still wasn't enough.

The kiss was wild and maddening at the same time, and she strained to get closer to him, desperate for something she couldn't name. Something just out of reach—

And when he set her away from him, with a dark little laugh, she thought she might die.

Then thought that death would be an excellent escape when reality hit her.

Because she was a disheveled mess on the floor of her office, staring up at the man who'd made her this way.

Perilously close to begging for things she couldn't even put into words.

She expected him to taunt her. To tell her she was a liar again, and remind her of all the ways he just proved it.

But Dominik stayed where he was, those gray eyes of his shuttered as he gazed back at her.

And she knew it was as good as admitting a weakness out loud, but she lifted her fingers and pressed them to her lips, not sure how she'd spent so many years on this earth without recognizing the way her own flesh could be used against her. And then tingle in the aftermath, like it wasn't enough.

As if she was sexual, after all.

"The company maintains a small number of corporate flats in this building," she managed to tell him when she'd composed herself a little, and she didn't sound like herself. She sounded like a prerecorded version of the woman she'd been when she'd left these offices to fly to Hungary. She wasn't sure she had access to that woman anymore. She wasn't sure she knew what had become of her.

But she was very sure that the creature she was now, right there at his feet, would be the undoing of her.

Assuming it wasn't already too late.

She climbed off the floor with as much dignity as she could muster. For the first time in her life, she cursed the fact that she wore such ridiculous shoes, with such high heels, that it was impossible to feel steady even when she was standing.

Right, a little voice inside her murmured archly. *Blame the shoes. It's definitely the* shoes.

"Corporate flats," he repeated after another long moment, that dark gaze all over her. "How...antiseptic."

But when she called down to the security desk to have one of the guards come and escort him there, he didn't argue.

Lauren told herself that she liked the space he left behind him. That it wasn't any kind of emptiness, but room for her to breathe.

And once she was alone, there was no one to see her when she sank down into her chair behind her desk, where she had always felt the most competent. There was no one to watch as she buried her face in her hands—still too hot, and no doubt too revealing—and let all those emotions she refused to look at and couldn't name spill down her cheeks at last.

CHAPTER EIGHT

BY MORNING SHE'D pulled herself together. The tears of the night before seemed to have happened to someone else. Someone far more fragile than Lauren had ever been, particularly in the crisp light of day. She showered in the bathroom off the executive suite, rinsing away any leftover emotion as well as the very long previous day, and changed into one of the complete outfits she kept at the office precisely for mornings like this.

Well. Perhaps not *precisely* like this. She didn't often plan and execute her own wedding. She'd worn her highest, most impractical pair of heels as a kind of tribute. And she was absolutely not thinking—much less overthinking—about the many questionable bargains she'd made with the strange man she'd found in the forest.

She knocked briskly on the door to the corporate flat at half nine on the dot, aware as she did that she didn't expect him to answer. A man as feral as Dominik was as likely to have disappeared in the night as a stray cat, surely—

But the door swung open. And Dominik stood there, dressed in nothing but a pair of casual trousers slung low on his hips, showing off acres and acres of...*him*.

For a moment—or possibly an hour—Lauren couldn't seem to do anything but gape at him.

"Did you imagine I would run off in the night?" he asked, reading her mind yet again. And not the most embarrassing part, for a change. She tried to swallow past the dryness in her throat. She tried to stop staring at all those ridges and planes and astonishing displays of honed male flesh. "I might have, of course, but there were restrictions in place."

She followed him inside the flat, down the small hall to the efficient kitchen, bright in the morning's summer sunlight. "You mean the security guards?"

He rounded the small counter and then regarded her over his coffee, strong enough that she could smell the rich aroma and blacker than sin. "I mean, Lauren, the fact I gave you my word."

Lauren had allowed sensation and emotion

and all that nonsense to get the best of her last night, but that was over now. It had to be, no matter how steady that gray gaze of his was. Or the brushfires it kicked up inside her, from the knot in her belly to the heat in her cheeks. So she cleared her throat and waved the tablet she carried in his direction, completely ignoring the tiny little hint of something bright like shame that wiggled around in all the knots she seemed to be made of today.

"I've sorted everything out," she told him, aware that she sounded as pinched and knotted as she felt. "We will marry in an hour."

Dominik didn't change expression and still, she felt as if he was laughing at her.

"And me without my pretty dress," he drawled.

"The vicar is a friend of the Combe family," she said as if she hadn't heard him. And she had to order herself not to fuss with her own dress, a simple little shift that was perfect for the office. And would do for a fake wedding, as well. "I took the liberty of claiming that ours is a deep and abiding love that requires a special license and speed, so it would be best all round if you do not dispute that."

"I had no intention of disputing it," Dominik said in that dark, sardonic voice of his that made her feel singed. "After all, I am nothing but a simple, lonely hermit, good for nothing but following the orders of wealthy aristocrats who cannot be bothered to attend the fake weddings they insisted occur in the first place. I am beside myself with joy and anticipation that I, too, can serve your master from afar in whatever way he sees fit. Truly, this is the family I dreamed of when I was a child in the orphanage."

He displayed his joy and anticipation by letting that impossible mouth of his crook, very slightly, in one corner, and Lauren hated that it felt like a punch. Directly into her gut.

"It is the romance of it all that makes my heart beat faster, little red," Dominik continued, sounding very nearly merry. If she overlooked that hard gleam in his eyes. "If you listen, I am certain you can hear it."

Lauren placed her tablet down on the marble countertop in a manner that could only be described as pointed. Or perhaps aggressive. But she kept her eyes on Dominik as if he really was some kind of wolf. As if looking away—for even an instant—could be the death of her.

And it wasn't his heart that she could hear, pounding loud enough to take down the nearest wall. It was hers.

"Could you take this seriously?" she demanded. "Could you at least try?"

He studied her for another moment as he lifted his coffee to his mouth and took a deep pull. "I didn't run off in the night as I assure you I could have done if I wished, regardless of what laughable corporate security you think was in place. The vicar bears down on us even as we speak. How much more seriously do you imagine I can take this?"

"You agreed to do this, repeatedly. I'm not sure that *I* agreed to submit myself to your... commentary."

She didn't expect that smile of his, bright and fierce. "Believe me, Lauren, there are all manner of things you might find yourself submitting to over the course of this day. Do not sell yourself short."

And she hated when he did that. When he said things in that voice of his, and they swirled around inside her—heat and madness and something like hope—making it clear that he was referring to all those dark and thorny things that she didn't understand.

That she didn't *want* to understand, she told herself stoutly.

"I've already agreed," she reminded him, with more ferocity than was strictly required. But she couldn't seem to bite it back. She had always been in such control of herself that she'd never learned how to *take* control of herself. If there were steps toward becoming composed, she didn't know them, and she could blame that on Dominik, too. "There's no need for all these insinuations."

"You've agreed? I thought it was I who agreed. To everything. Like a house pet on a chain."

His voice was mild but his gaze was…not.

"You asked me for a wedding night," she reminded him, her heart still pounding like it wanted to knock her flat. "And you know that I keep my promises. Every time you've asked to kiss me, I've allowed it."

"Surrendered to it, one might even say, with notable enthusiasm. Once you get started."

"My point," she said through her teeth, not certain why she was suddenly so angry, only that she couldn't seem to keep it inside her, where she was shaky and too hot and not the least bit *composed*, "is that you don't have to continue with all the veiled references. Or even the euphemisms. You demanded sex in return for marrying me, and I agreed to give it to you. The end."

It was a simple statement of fact, she thought. There was no reason at all that he should stare at her that way as if he was stripping all the air from the flat. From the world.

"If it is so distasteful to you, Lauren, don't."

But his voice was too smooth. Too silky. And all she could hear was the undercurrent beneath it, which roared through her like an impenetrable wall of flame.

"Don't?" she managed to echo. "Is that an option?"

"While you are busy marinating in the injustice of it all, remind yourself that it is not I who tracked you down in the middle of a forest, then dragged you back to England. If I wish to go through with a sham marriage for the sheer pleasure of the wedding night you will provide me as lure, that is my business." Dominik tilted his head slightly to one side. "Perhaps you should ask yourself what you are willing to do for a paycheck. And why."

"It's a little more complicated than that."

"Is it? Maybe it is time you ask yourself what you *wouldn't* do if your Mr. Combe asked it. You may find the answers illuminating."

"You obviously enjoy keeping to yourself." Lauren wasn't sure why all that breathless fury wound around and around inside her, or why she wanted nothing more than to throw it at him. She only wished she could be sure of her aim. "But some people prefer to be on a team."

"The team that is currently enjoying a holiday in scenic Australia? Or the one left here with a list of instructions and a heretofore unknown half brother to civilize through the glorious institution of marriage?" He smirked. "Go team."

Her jaw ached and she realized, belatedly, that she was clenching her teeth. *"You agreed."*

"So I did." And all he was doing was standing there across a block of marble, so there was no reason he should make her feel so... dizzy. "But then again, so did you. Is that what this is about, little red? Are you so terrified of the things you promised me?"

That took the wind out of her as surely as if she'd fallen hard and landed worse.

"What does it matter if I'm terrified or not?" She only realized after she'd said it that it was as good as an admission. "Would it change your mind?"

"It might change my approach," he said, that gleaming, dark thing in his gaze again, and she didn't understand how or why it connected to all that breathlessness inside her.

Almost as if it wasn't *fury* at all. "Then again, it might not."

"In any case, congratulations are in order," she managed to say, feeling battered for no good reason at all. "In short order you will have a wife. And shortly after that, a wedding night sacrifice, like something out of the history books."

He laughed, rich and deep, and deeper when she scowled at him. "Do you think to shame me, Lauren? There are any number of men who might stand before you and thunder this way and that about how they dislike the taste of martyrdom in their beds, but not me."

"I am somehow unsurprised."

Dominik didn't move and yet, again, Lauren felt as if he surrounded her. As if those hands of his might as well have been all over her. She felt as if they were.

"You're not terrified of me," he said with a quiet certainty that made her shake. "You're terrified of yourself. And all those things you told yourself you don't know how to feel." That laughter was still all over his face, but his gray gaze made her feel pinned to the floor where she stood. "You're terrified that you'll wake up tomorrow so alive with feeling you won't know who you are."

"Either that or even more bored than I am

right now," she said, though her throat felt scraped raw with all the things she didn't say. Or scream.

"Yes, so deeply bored," he said, and laughed again. Then he leaned forward until he rested his elbows on the countertop between them, making it impossible to pretend she didn't see the play of his muscles beneath the acres and acres of smooth male skin that he'd clearly shared with the sun in that Hungarian clearing. "But tell me this, Lauren. Does your boredom make you wet?"

For a moment she couldn't process the question. She couldn't understand it.

Then she did, and a tide of red washed over her, igniting her from the very top of her head to the tender spaces between her toes. No one had ever asked her a question like that. She hadn't known, until right now, that people really discussed such things in the course of an otherwise more or less regular day. She told herself she was horrified. Disgusted. She told herself she didn't even know what he meant, only that it was vile. That *he* was.

But she did know what he meant.

And she was molten straight through, red hot and flush with it, and decidedly not bored.

"You have twenty minutes," she told him

when she could be sure her voice was clipped and cold again. "I trust you will be ready?"

"I will take that as a yes," he rumbled at her, entirely too male and much too sure of himself. "You are so wet you can hardly stand still. Don't worry, little red. You might not know what to do about that. But I do."

He straightened, then rounded the counter. Lauren pulled herself taut and rigid as if he was launching an attack—then told herself it was sheer relief that wound its way through her when he made no move toward her at all. He headed toward the flat's bedroom instead.

"You're welcome to join me in the shower," he said over his shoulder, and she didn't have to see his face to know he was laughing at her. "If you dare."

And she was still standing right where he'd left her when she heard the water go on. Frozen solid at the edge of the counter with her hands in fists, curled up so tight her nails were digging into her palms.

She made herself uncurl her fingers, one at a time. She made herself breathe, shoving back the temper and the fury until she could see what was beneath it.

And see that once again, he was right. It was fear.

Not of him. But of herself.

And how very much she wanted to see, at last, what it was she'd been missing all this time.

That was the thought that had kept sneaking into her head over the course of the long night.

She'd hardly slept, there on that couch in her office where she spent more time than she ever had in the flat she shared with Mary. And Lauren had always prided herself on not feeling the things that others did. She'd congratulated herself on not being dragged into the same emotional quagmires they always were. It made her better at doing her job. It made it easier to navigate the corporate world.

But Dominik had forced her to face the fact that she *could* feel all kinds of things, she just…hadn't.

Lauren had spent so long assuring herself she didn't want the things she couldn't feel. Or couldn't have. Her parents' love, the happy families they made without her, the sorts of romantic and sexual relationships all her friends and colleagues were forever falling in and out of with such abandon. She'd told anyone who asked that she wasn't built for those sorts of entanglements.

Secretly, she'd always believed she was

above them. That she was better than all that mess and regret.

But one day of kissing Dominik James on demand and she was forced to wonder—if it wasn't about better or worse, but about meeting someone who made her feel things she hadn't thought she could, where did that leave her except woefully inexperienced? And frozen in amber on a shelf of her own making?

Lauren didn't like that thought at all. She ran her hands over her sensible shift dress, her usual office wear, and tried to pretend that she wasn't shaking.

But what if you melted? whispered a voice deep inside her that she'd never heard before, layered with insinuation and something she was terribly afraid might be grief. *What if you let Dominik melt you as he pleased?*

She let out a breath she hadn't known she was holding. And she swayed on her feet, yet knew full well it wasn't because of the skyscraper height of her shoes.

And she entertained a revolutionary thought. If she had to do this, anyway—if she was going to marry this man, and stay married to him for as long as it took to ride out the public's interest in yet another family scandal—shouldn't she take it as an opportunity?

She already knew that Dominik could make her feel things that she never had before. And yes, that was overwhelming. A mad, wild whirl that she hardly knew how to process. Especially when she'd been certain, all her life, that she wasn't capable of such things.

Maybe she didn't know how to want. But it had never occurred to her before now that she hadn't been born that way. That maybe, just maybe, that was because no one had ever wanted her—especially the people who should have wanted her the most.

She didn't know why Dominik wanted to play these games with her, but he did. He clearly did, or he wouldn't be here. Lauren was persuasive, but she knew full well she couldn't have forced that man to do a single thing he didn't want to do.

So why shouldn't she benefit, too?

She had spent a lot of time and energy telling herself that she didn't care that she was so clearly different from everyone else she met. That she was somehow set apart from the rest of the human race, unmoved by their passions and their baser needs. But what if she wasn't?

What if she wasn't an alien, after all?

That was what one of her kissing experiments had called her when she had declined his offer to take their experiment in a more horizontal direction. Among other, less savory names and accusations.

Just as Dominik had called her a robot.

What if she...wasn't?

What if she melted, after all?

Lauren waited until he reemerged from his bedchamber, dressed in a crisp, dark suit that confused her, it was so well-made. His hair was tamed, pushed back from his face, and he'd even shaved, showing off the cut line of his ruthlessly masculine jaw. He looked like what he was—the eldest son of the current generation of San Giacomos. But she couldn't concentrate on any of the surprisingly sophisticated male beauty he threw around him like light, because she knew that if she didn't say what she wanted right here and now, she never would.

"I will give you a wedding night," she told him.

"So we have already agreed," he said in that silky way of his that made her whole body turn to jelly. And her stomach doing flips inside her didn't exactly help. "Is this a renegotiation of terms?"

"If it takes more than one night, that's all right," she forced herself to tell him, though it made her feel queasy. And light-headed. Especially when he stopped tugging at his shirt cuffs and transferred all his considerable attention to her. "I want to learn."

"Learn what?"

And maybe his voice wasn't particularly, dangerously quiet. Maybe it just sounded like that in her head, next to all that roaring.

"Everyone has all this sex," she said, the words crashing through her and out of her. She couldn't control them. She couldn't do anything but throw them across the room like bombs. "People walk around *consumed* by it, and I want to know why. I don't just mean I want you to take my virginity, though you will. And that's fine."

"I'm delighted to hear you're on board," he said drily, though it was the arrested sort of gleam in his eyes that she couldn't seem to look away from. Because it made her feel as if a great wind was blowing, directly at her, and there was nothing she could do to stop it. "No one likes an unenthusiastic deflowering. Gardening metaphors aside, it's really not all that much fun. Anyone who tells you otherwise has never had the pleasure. Or any pleasure, I can only assume."

"I have no idea what you're on about." He looked even more taken aback by that, and she moved toward him—then thought better of it, as putting herself in arm's reach of this man had yet to end well for her. Even if that was her current goal. "I want to understand why people *yearn.* I want to understand what all the fuss is about. Why people—you among them—look at me like something's wrong with me if I say I'm not interested in it. Can you do that, Dominik?"

Maybe it was the first time she'd called him by his name. She wasn't sure, but she felt as if it was. And he looked at her as if she'd struck him.

"I've spent my whole life never quite understanding the people around me." And Lauren knew she would be horrified—later—that her voice broke then, showing her hand. Telling him even more than she'd wanted. "Never really getting the joke. Or the small, underlying assumptions that people make about the world because of these feelings they cart about with them wherever they go. I never got those, either. Just once I want to know what the big secret is. I want to know what all the songs are about. I want to know what so many parents feel they need to protect their children from. I want to *know.*"

"Lauren..."

And she didn't recognize that look on his

face then. Gone was the mocking, sardonic gleam in his eyes. The theatrics, the danger. The challenge.

She was terribly afraid that what she was seeing was pity, and she thought that might kill her.

"I know this is all a game to you," she said hurriedly, before he could crush her, and had that out-of-body feeling again. As if she was watching herself from far away, and couldn't do a single thing to stop the words that kept pouring out of her mouth. "Maybe you have your own dark reasons for wanting to do what Mr. Combe wants, and I don't blame you. Family dynamics are difficult enough when you've known the players all your life. But you said that there could be certain things that were between the two of us. That are only ours. And I want this to be one of them." Her heart was in her throat and she couldn't swallow it down. She could only hope she didn't choke on it. "I want to know *why*."

He straightened then, and she couldn't read the expression he wore. Arrested, still. But there was a different light in those near-silver eyes of his. He held out his hand, that gray gaze steady on hers, as if that alone could hold her up.

She believed it.

Lauren was tempted to call the way he was looking at her *kind.* And she had absolutely no idea why that should make her want to cry. Or how she managed to keep from doing just that when her sight blurred.

"Come," Dominik said, his voice gruff and sure as if he was already reciting his vows before the vicar. And more shocking by far, as if those vows meant something to him. "Marry me, little red, and I will teach you."

CHAPTER NINE

WHEN HE LOOKED back on this episode and cataloged his mistakes—something Dominik knew he would get to as surely as night followed day—he would trace it all back to the fatal decision to step outside his cabin and wait for the Englishwoman the innkeeper had called from town to tell him was headed his way.

It had seemed so innocuous at the time. No one ever visited his cabin, with or without an invitation, and he hadn't known what would come of entertaining the whims of the one woman who had dared come find him. He'd been curious. Especially when he'd seen her, gold hair gleaming and that red cloak flowing around her like a premonition.

How could he have known?

And now Dominik found himself in exactly the sort of stuffy, sprawling, stately home he most despised, with no one to blame but himself. Combe Manor sat high on a ridge overlooking the Yorkshire village that had once housed the mills that had provided the men who'd lived in this house a one-way ticket out of their humble beginnings.

They had built Combe Manor and started Combe Industries. Dominik had also fought his way out of a rocky, unpleasant start…but he'd chosen to hoard his wealth and live off by himself in the middle of the woods.

Dominik felt like an imposter. Because he was an imposter.

He might have shared blood with the distant aristocrat he'd seen on the screen in a London office, but he didn't share…this. Ancient houses filled with the kind of art and antiques that spoke of wealth that went far beyond the bank. It was nearly two centuries of having more. Of having everything, for that matter. It was generations of men who had stood where he did now, staring out the windows in a library filled with books only exquisitely educated men read, staring down at the village where, once upon a time, other men scurried about adding to the Combe coffers.

And he knew that the Combe family was brand-spanking-new in terms of wealth when stood next to the might and historic reach of the San Giacomos.

Dominik might share that blood, but he was an orphan. A street kid who'd lived rough for years and had done what was necessary to feed himself, keep himself clothed and find shelter. A soldier who had done his duty and followed his orders, and had found himself in situations he never mentioned when civilians were near.

Blood was nothing next to the life he'd lived. And he was surprised this fancy, up-itself house didn't fall down around his ears.

But when he heard the soft click of much too high heels against the floor behind him, he turned.

Almost as if he couldn't help himself.

Because the house still stood despite the fact he was here, polluting it. And more astonishing still, the woman who walked toward him, her blond hair shining and a wary look on her pretty face, was his wife.

His wife.

The ceremony, such as it was, had gone smoothly. The vicar had arrived right on time, and they had recited their vows in a pretty sort of boardroom high on top of the London building that housed his half brother's multinational business. Lauren had produced rings, proving that she did indeed think of everything, they had exchanged them and that was that.

Dominik was not an impulsive man. Yet, he had gone ahead and married a woman for the hell of it.

And he was having trouble remembering what *the hell of it* was, because all he could seem to think about was Lauren. And more specific, helping Lauren out of those impossible heels she wore. Peeling that sweet little dress off her curves, and then finally—*finally*—doing something about this intense, unreasonable hunger for her that had been dogging him since the moment he'd laid eyes on her.

The moment he'd stepped out of the shadows of his own porch and had put all of this into motion.

There had been no reception. Lauren had taken a detour to her office that had turned into several hours of work. Afterward she had herded him into another sleek, black car, then back to the same plane, which they'd flown for a brief little hop to the north of England. Another car ride from the airfield and here they were in an echoing old mausoleum that had been erected to celebrate and flatter the kinds of men Dominik had always hated.

It had never crossed his mind that he was one of them. He'd never wanted to be one of them.

And the fact he'd found out he was the very thing he loathed didn't change a thing. He couldn't erase the life he'd led up to this point. He couldn't pretend he'd had a different life now that he was being offered his rich mother's guilt in the form of an identity that meant nothing to him.

But it was difficult to remember the hard line he planned to take when this woman—his *wife*, to add another impossibility to the pile—stood before him.

"I have just spoken to Mr. Combe," she began, because, of course, she'd been off the moment they'd set foot in this house. Dominik had welcomed the opportunity to ask himself what on earth he was doing here while she'd busied herself with more calls and emails and tasks that apparently needed doing *at once*.

And Dominik had made any number of mistakes already. There was the speaking to her in the first place that he would have to unpack at some later date, when all of this was behind him. Besides, he'd compounded that error, time and again. He should never have touched her. He should certainly never have kissed her. He should have let her fly off back to London on her own, and he certainly, without any doubt, should never have married her.

The situation would almost be funny if it wasn't so...preposterous.

But one thing Dominik knew beyond a shadow of any doubt. He did not want to hear about his damned brother again. Not tonight.

"Do me this one favor, please," he said in a voice that came out as more of a growl than he'd intended. Or maybe it was exactly the growl that was called for, he thought, when her eyes widened. "This is our wedding night. We have a great many things to accomplish, you and I. Why don't we leave your Mr. Combe where he belongs—across the planet, doing whatever it is he does that requires you to do five times as much in support."

He expected her to argue. He was sure he could see the start of it kicking up all over her lovely face and in the way she held her shoulders so tight and high.

But she surprised him.

She held his gaze, folded her hands in front of her and inclined her head.

Giving him what he wanted.

And the same demon that had spurred him

on from the start—pushing him to walk out onto that porch and start all of this in the first place—sat up inside him, clearly not as intimidated by a stately library and a grand old house the way he was.

"What's this?" he asked quietly. "Is that all it took to tame you, little red? A ring on your finger and a few vows in front of the vicar? That's all that was required to make you soft? Yielding? Obedient?"

She made a sound that could as easily have been a cough as a laugh. "I am not certain I would call myself any of those things, no matter what jewelry I wear on my fingers. But I agreed to the wedding night. And... whatever else. I have every intention of going through with it."

"You make it sound so appealing." He eyed her, not sure if he was looking for her weaknesses or better yet, the places she was likely to be most sensitive. "You could do worse than a little softness. Yielding will make it sweeter for the both of us. And obedience, well..."

He grinned at that, as one image after the next chased through his head.

"I've never been much good at that, either, I'm afraid." She said it with such confidence, tipping her chin up to go with it. And more than that, pride. "If you're looking for obedience, I'm afraid you're in for some disappointment."

"You cannot truly believe you are not obedient." He moved toward her, leaving the window—and its view of the ruins of the mills that had built this place—behind him. "You obey one man because he pays you. What will it take, I wonder, for you to obey your husband with even a portion of that dedication?"

And he had the distinct pleasure of watching her shiver, goose bumps telling him her secrets as they rippled to life on her skin.

He was so hard he thought it might hurt him.

Dominik crossed the vast expanse of the library floor until he was in front of her, and then he kept moving, wandering in a lazy circle around her as if she was on an auction block and he was the buyer.

Another image that pulsed in him like need.

"I asked you to teach me." And he could hear all the nerves crackling in her voice. As obvious as the goose bumps down the length of her arms. "Does that come with extra doses of humiliation or is that merely an add-on extra?"

"It's my lesson to teach, Lauren. Why don't you stop trying to top from the bottom?"

He'd made a full circle around her then, and faced her once more. And he reveled in the look on her face. Wariness and expectation. That sweet pink flush.

And a certain hectic awareness in her caramel-colored eyes.

She was without doubt the most beautiful woman he had ever seen. And she was his.

She had made herself his.

"What do you want me to do?" Lauren asked, her voice the softest he'd ever heard it.

He reached out to smooth his hand over all her gleaming blond hair, still pulled back in that sleek, professional ponytail. He considered that tidy ponytail part of her armor.

And he wanted none of that armor between them. Not tonight.

"It's time to play Rapunzel," he told her. When she only stared back at him, he tugged on the ponytail, just sharp enough to make her hitch in a breath. "Let down your hair, little red."

He watched the pulse in her throat kick into high gear. Her flush deepened, and he was fairly certain she'd moved into holding her breath.

But she obeyed him all the same, reaching

back to tug the elastic out of her hair. When it was loose she ran her free hand through the mass of it, letting it fall where it would, thick and gold and smelling of apples.

She kept saying she didn't believe in fairy tales, but Dominik was sure he'd ended up in the midst of one all the same. And he knew the price of taking a bite out of a sweet morsel like Lauren, a golden-haired princess as innocent as she was sweet to look upon, but he didn't care. Bake him into a pie, turn him into stone—he meant to have this woman.

He made a low, rumbling sound of approval, because with her hair down she looked different. Less sharp. Less sleek. More accessible. The hair tumbled over her shoulders and made her seem…very nearly romantic.

Dominik remembered the things he'd promised her, and that ache in him grew sharper and more insistent by the second, so he simply bent and scooped her up into his arms.

She let out the breath she'd been holding in a kind of gasp, but he was already moving. He held her high against his chest, a soft, sweet weight in his arms, and after a startled moment she snuck her arms around his neck.

And that very nearly undid him.

The sort of massive, theatrical staircase that had never made sense to him dominated the front hall, and he took the left side, heading upstairs.

"Oh, the guest suites are actually—" she began, shifting in his arms and showing him that frown of hers he liked far too much.

"Is anyone else here?"

He already knew the answer. She had told him the house was empty when they'd landed in Yorkshire. She'd told him a lot of information about the house, the grounds, the village, the distant moors and mountains—as if she'd believed what he truly wanted today was a travelogue and a lecture on the Combe family.

"You know that Mr. Combe is in Australia, and his sister, Pia—" She cut herself off, her gaze locking to his. "Well. She's your sister, too, of course. And she is currently in the kingdom of Atilia."

"The island."

"Yes, it's actually several islands in the Ionian Sea—"

"I don't care." He didn't. Not about Matteo Combe or Pia Combe or anything at all but the woman in his arms. "How many beds are there in a house like this?"

"Fifteen," she replied, her gaze searching his. Then widening as he smiled.

"Never fear, Lauren. I intend to christen them all."

He took the first door he found, carrying her into a sprawling sitting room that led, eventually, into an actual bedroom. The bed itself was a massive thing, as if they'd chopped down trees that could have been the masts of ships to make all four posters, but Dominik found his normal disgust about class issues faded in the face of all the lovely possibilities.

There were just so many things an imaginative man could do with bedposts and a willing woman.

He set her down at the side of the bed and smiled wider when she had to reach out to steady herself. "Those shoes may well be the death of you. It is the shoes, is it not? And not something else entirely that leaves you so… unbalanced?"

She shot him a look, but she didn't say anything. She reached down, fiddled with the buckle around one delicate ankle, then kicked her shoe off. She repeated it on the other side, and when she was done she was nearly a foot shorter.

And then she smiled up at him, her gaze as full of challenge as it was of wariness.

"I didn't realize all the witty banter came

as part of the package. I thought it would just be, you know, straight to it. No discussion."

"You could have gotten that in any pub you've ever set foot in with precious little effort on your part."

He shrugged out of the formal suit jacket he'd been wearing all day, like the trained monkey he'd allowed himself to become. And he was well aware of the convulsive way she swallowed, her gaze following his shoulders as if she couldn't bring herself to look away from him.

Dominik liked that a little too much. "Why didn't you?"

He started on his buttons then, one after the next, unable to keep his lips from quirking as she followed his fingers as they moved down his chest. And took much too long to raise her gaze back to his.

"Pardon?"

"If you were curious about experimenting with your nonsexual nature, Lauren, why not get off with a stranger after a few drinks? I think you'll find it's a tried and true method employed by people everywhere."

"As appealing as that sounds, I was never curious before. I was never curious before—"

She looked stricken the moment the words were out. And the word she'd been about to say hung between them as surely as if she'd shouted it. *You.*

I was never curious before you.

And Dominik felt...hushed. Something like humbled.

"Don't worry," he found himself saying, though his voice was gruff and he'd planned to be so much more smooth, more in control, hadn't he? "I promise you will enjoy this far more than a drunken fumble in the toilets after too much liquid courage and a pair of beer goggles."

She blinked as if she was imagining that, and Dominik didn't want a single thing in her head but him.

He tossed his shirt aside, then nodded at her. "Your dress, wife. Take it off."

Her breath shuddered out of her, and her hands trembled when she reached down to grip the hem of the shift dress she wore. She had to wiggle as she lifted it, peeling it up and off and displaying herself to him as she went.

Inch by luscious inch.

At last, he thought as she tossed the dress aside and stood there before him wearing nothing but a delicate lace bra that cupped her perfect breasts, and a pair of pale pink panties that gleamed a bit in the last of the light of the waning summer afternoon.

She made his mouth water.

And God, how she made him ache.

He reached over and put his hands on her, finally. He drew her hair over her shoulders, then followed the line of each arm. Down to find her fingers, particularly the one that wore his ring, then back up again. He found the throat where her pulse pounded out a rhythm he could feel in the hardest part of him, and each soft swell of her breast above the fabric that covered them and held them aloft.

She was like poured cream, sweet and rich, and so soft to the touch he had to bite back a groan. He traced his way over the tempting curve of her belly, her hips made for his hands, and then behind to her pert bottom.

She was warm already, but she became hot beneath his palms.

And he was delighted to find that when she flushed, she turned bright red all the way down to her navel. Better by far than he'd imagined.

He dropped to his knees, wrapped his arms around her and dropped his mouth to a spot just below her navel, smiling when she jolted against him.

Because touching her wasn't enough. He wanted to taste her.

First, he retraced his steps, putting his mouth everywhere he could reach, relishing each shocked and greedy little noise she made. The way she widened her stance, then sagged back against the high bed as if her knees could no longer hold her. She buried her hands in his hair, but either she didn't know how to guide him, or didn't want to, so he made his own path.

And when her eyes looked blind with need, he reached up and unhooked her bra, carefully removing it so he could expose her breasts to his view.

Perfect. She was perfect, and he leaned in close so he could take his fill of her. He pulled one nipple deep into his mouth, sucking until she cried out.

And Dominik thought it was the most glorious sound he had ever heard.

When he was finished with both nipples, they stood harder and more proud. And she was gripping the bed sheets behind her, her head tipped back so all of her golden hair spread around her like a halo.

He shifted forward, lifting her up and setting her back on the bed so he could peel the panties from her hips.

As he pulled them down her satiny legs, she panted. And was making the slightest high-pitched sounds in the back of her throat, if he wasn't mistaken.

She only got louder when he lifted up her legs and set them on his shoulders so they dangled down his back, and then he lost himself in the fact he had full, unfettered access to all that molten sweetness between her legs.

The scent of her arousal roared in him, making him crazy.

Making him as close to desperate as he'd ever been.

He looked up and let his lips curve when he found her gazing back at him, a look of wonder on her face.

And something like disbelief in her eyes.

"You... My legs..." She hardly sounded like herself.

"All the better to eat you with, my dear," he said, dark and greedy.

And then he set his mouth to the core of her, and showed her exactly how real the fairy tales were, after all.

CHAPTER TEN

IT HIT HER like a punch, thick and deep, setting Lauren alight from the inside out.

It made her go rigid, then shake.

But that didn't stop Dominik.

Her husband.

He was licking into her as if he planned to go on forever. He was using the edge of his teeth, his wicked tongue and the scrape of his jaw. His shoulders kept her thighs apart, and he didn't seem to care that her hands were buried in his hair. And tugging.

And after the first punch, there was a different, deeper fire. A kind of dancing flame she hardly knew how to name, and then there was more.

A shattering.

As if there were new ways to burn, and Dominik was intent on showing her each and every one of them.

The third time she exploded, he pulled

his mouth away from her, pressing his lips against her inner thigh so she could feel him smile.

He stood, hauling her with him as he went, and then somehow they were both in the middle of a giant bed in one of the family's suites she had never dared enter on her previous trips to Combe Manor.

He rolled over her, and Lauren realized she must have lost time somewhere, because he was naked, too. She had no memory of him stripping off his trousers.

Not that she cared.

Because she could feel him everywhere, muscled legs between her, and the heat of his skin. All that lean weight of his. The crispness of the hair that dusted his decidedly male body. His eyes were like silver, hot and indulgent at once, and he braced himself over her as she ran her hands down all the planes and ridges of his beautiful chest, the way she'd wanted to since he'd opened the door this morning.

It was finally her turn to touch him. And she was determined to touch *all* of him, with all the fascination she hadn't know she held inside her. But there was no denying it as she followed her fingers wherever they wanted to go. There was no pretending it didn't swell and dance inside her.

"I don't understand how a man can be so beautiful," she whispered, and if that was betraying herself the way she feared it was, she couldn't bring herself to care about that.

Because he took her mouth then, a hard, mad claiming, and it thrilled her.

She surged against him, unable to get close enough. Unable to process each and every sensation that rolled over her, spiraled around inside her and made her want nothing more than to press every part of her against every part of him.

And she could feel it then. The hardest part of him, there between them. Velvet and steel, insistent against the soft skin of her belly.

It made her shudder all over again.

He slanted his mouth over hers, and then his hands were working magic between them. She heard the faint sound of foil, and then he settled himself between her legs as if all this time, her whole life, she had been made to hold him just like this.

Dominik had asked her if she was wet before. And now she knew what he meant in an entirely different way.

But he growled his approval as his fingers found the neediest part of her, playing with her until she bucked against him, her head thrashing back against the mattress.

He lifted her knees, then settled himself even more completely between them, so he was flush against her.

"Tell me if you don't feel anything," he said, his voice nearly unrecognizable, there at her ear.

"If I don't..." she began.

But then she could feel him, there at her center.

He pressed against the resistance he found; her body protested enough to make her wince, and then it was over.

Or just beginning, really.

Because he kept pressing. In and in, and there was too much. She couldn't name the things she felt; she could barely experience them as they happened—

"Remember," and his voice was a growl again. "You are nonsexual, little red. You do not feel what others do. Is that how this feels?"

But she couldn't answer him.

She couldn't do anything but dig her fingers into his shoulders as he opened her, pressed deeper and stretched her farther still.

Then finally, and yet too soon, he stopped.

And for a moment he only gazed down at

her, propped up on his elbows with nothing but silver in his gaze and that very nearly stern set to his mouth.

While he was buried completely within her body.

And the knowledge of that, mixed with the exquisite sensation, so full and so deep, made her break apart all over again.

Less like a fist this time, and more like a wave. Over and over, until it wore itself out against the shore.

And when she opened her eyes again, she could see Dominik's jaw clenched tight and something harder in his gaze. Determination, perhaps.

"You're killing me," he gritted out.

She tried to catch her breath. "Am I doing it wrong?"

And he let out a kind of sigh, or maybe it was a groan, and he dropped down to gather her even more firmly beneath him.

"No, little red, you're not doing it wrong."

But she thought he sounded tortured as he said it.

Then Lauren couldn't care about that, either, because he began to move.

And it was everything she'd never known she wanted. She had never known she could want at all. It was the difference between a dark, cloudy sky, and a canopy of stars.

And she couldn't breathe. She couldn't *think*. She could only feel.

She was all sensation. All greed and passion, longing and desire, and all of it focused on the man who moved within her, teaching her with every thrust.

About need. About want.

About everything she had been missing, all these lonely years.

He taught her about hope, and he taught her about wonder, and still he kept on.

Lesson after lesson, as each thrust made it worse. Better.

As he made her undeniably human, flesh and passion made real, as surely as any kiss in a fairy tale story.

Until there was nothing between them but fire.

The glory of flames that danced and consumed them, made them one, and changed everything.

And when she exploded that time, he went with her.

He shouldn't have gone out on that porch, Dominik thought grimly a long while later as the sky outside darkened to a mysterious deep blue, and Lauren lay sprawled against his chest, her breathing even and her eyes closed.

He should have stayed in Hungary. He should have laughed off the notion that he was an heir to anything.

And he never, ever should have suggested that they make this marriage real.

He felt...wrecked.

And yet he couldn't seem to bring himself to shift her off him. It would be easy enough to do. A little roll, and he could leave her here. He could leave behind this great house and all its obnoxious history. He could pretend he truly didn't care about the woman who'd rid herself of him, then later chosen this.

But he had promised to take part in this whole charade, hadn't he? He'd promised not only to marry Lauren, but to subject himself to the rest of it, too. Hadn't she mentioned comportment? The press?

It was his own fault that he'd ended up here. He accepted that.

But he could honestly say that it had never occurred to him that sex with Lauren could possibly be this...ruinous.

Devastating, something in him whispered.

He hadn't imagined that anything could get

to him. Nothing had in years. And no woman had ever come close.

Dominik had never experienced the overwhelming sensation that he wasn't only naked in the sense of having no clothes on—he was naked in every sense. Transparent with it, so anyone who happened by could see all the things in him he'd learned to pack away, out of view. First, as an orphan who had to try his best to act perfect for prospective parents. Then as a kid on the street who had to act tough enough to be left alone. Then as a soldier who had to act as if nothing he was ordered to do stayed with him.

And he couldn't say he much cared for the sensation now.

He needed to get up and leave this bed. He needed to go for a long, punishing run to clear his head. He needed to do something physical until he took the edge off all the odd things swirling around inside him, showing too much as if she'd knocked down every last boundary he had, and Dominik certainly couldn't allow that—

But she stirred then, shifting all that smooth, soft heat against him, and a new wave of intense heat washed over him.

She let out a sigh that sounded like his name, and what was he supposed to do with that?

Despite himself, he held on to her.

Especially when she lifted her head, piled her hands beneath her chin and blinked up at him.

And the things he wanted to say appalled him.

He cleared his throat. "Do you feel sufficiently indoctrinated into the sport?"

He hardly recognized his own voice. Or that note in it that he was fairly certain was... playfulness? And his hands were on her curves as if he needed to assure himself that they were real. That she was.

"Is it a sport? I thought of it more as a pastime. A habit, perhaps." She considered it, and what was wrong with him that he enjoyed watching a woman *think*? "Or for some, I suppose, an addiction."

"There are always hobbyists and amateurs, little red," he found himself saying, a certain...*warmth* in his voice that he wanted to rip out with his own fingers. But he didn't know where to start. "But I have never counted myself among them."

He meant to leave, and yet his hands were on her, smoothing their way down her back, then cupping her bottom. He knew he needed to let her go and make sure this never happened again, but she was smiling.

And he hardly knew her. Gone was all that sharpness, and in its place was a kind of soft, almost dreamy expression that made his chest hurt.

As if she was the one teaching him a lesson here.

"I beg your pardon. I didn't realize I was addressing such a renowned star of the bedroom," she said, and her lovely eyes danced with laughter.

It only served to remind him that she didn't laugh nearly enough.

"I will excuse it," he told her. "Once."

He needed to put distance between them. Now. Dominik knew that the way he knew every other fact of his existence. He knew it like every single memory he had of the nuns. The streets. The missions he'd been sent on.

He wasn't a man built for connection. He didn't want to be the kind of man who could connect with people, because people were what was wrong with the world. People had built this house. A person had given him away. He wanted nothing to do with *people*, or he never would have taken himself off into the woods in the first place.

But this pretty, impossible person was looking at him as if he was the whole world, her cheeks heating into red blazes he couldn't keep from touching. He ran his knuckles over one, then the other, silky smooth and wildly hot.

"It is still our wedding night," she pointed out.

"So it is."

Lauren lowered her lashes, then traced a small pattern against his chest with one fingertip.

"I don't know how this works. Or if you can. Physically, I mean. But I wondered... I mean, I hoped..." She blew out a breath. "Was that the whole of the lesson?"

And Dominik was only a man, after all, no matter how he'd tried to make himself into a monster, out there in his forest. And the part of him that had been greedy for her since the moment he'd seen her could never be happy with so small a taste.

Will you ever be satisfied? a voice in him asked. *Or will you always want more?*

That should have sent him racing for the door. He needed to leave, right now, but he found himself lifting her against him instead. He drew her up on her knees so she straddled him, and watched as she looked down between them, blinked and then smiled.

Wickedly, God help him.

"By all means," he encouraged her, his hands on her hips. "Allow me to teach you something else I feel certain you won't feel, as shut off and uninterested in these things as you are."

She found him then, wrapping her hands around the hardest expression of his need and guiding him to the center of her heat.

As if she'd been born for this. For him.

"No," she murmured breathlessly. And then smiled as she took him inside her as if he'd been made to fit her so perfectly, just like that. "I don't expect I'll feel anything at all."

And there was nothing for it. There was no holding back.

Dominik gave himself over to his doom.

CHAPTER ELEVEN

THE SITUATION DID not improve as the days slid by and turned inevitably into weeks.

Dominik needed to put a stop to the madness. There was no debate on that topic. The pressing need to leave the mess he'd made here, get the hell out of England, and away from the woman he never should have married, beat in him like a drum. It was the first thing he thought of when he woke. It dogged him through the long summer days. It even wormed its way into his dreams.

But one day led into the next, and he went nowhere. He didn't even try to leave as if he was the one who'd wandered into the wrong forest and found himself under some kind of spell he couldn't break.

Meanwhile, they traded lesson for lesson.

"I know how to use utensils, little red," he told her darkly one morning after he'd come back from a punishing run—yet not punishing enough, clearly, as he'd returned to Combe Manor—and had showered and changed only to find the formal dining room set with acres of silver on either side of each plate. There was a mess of glasses and extra plates everywhere he looked.

And Lauren sat there with her hair pulled back into the smooth ponytail he took personally and that prissy look on her face.

The very same prissy look that made him hard and greedy for her, instantly.

"This won't be a lesson about basic competence with a fork, which I'll go ahead and assume you mastered some time ago," she told him tartly. Her gaze swept over him, making him feel as if he was still that grubby-faced orphan, never quite good enough. He gritted his teeth against it, because that was the last thing he needed. The present was complicated enough without dragging in the past. "This will be about formal manners for formal dinners."

"Alternatively, I could cook for myself, eat with own my fingers if I so desire and continue to have the exact same blood in my veins that I've always had with no one the least bit interested either way. None of this matters."

He expected her to come back at him, sharp

and amusing, but she didn't. She studied him for a moment instead, and he still didn't know how to handle the way she looked at him these days. It was softer. Warmer.

It was too dangerous. It scraped at him until he felt raw and he could never get enough of it, all the same.

"It depends on your perspective, I suppose," she said. "It's not rocket science, of course. The fate of the world doesn't hang in the balance. History books won't be written about what fork you use at a banquet. But the funny thing about manners is that they can often stand in for the things you lack."

"And what is it I lack, exactly? Be specific, please. I dare you."

"I'm talking about me, Dominik. Not you."

And when she smiled, the world stopped.

He told himself it was one more sign he needed to get away from her. Instead, he took the seat opposite her at the table as if he really was under her spell.

Why couldn't he break it?

"When I was nine my parents had been divorced for two years, which means each of them was married again. My stepmother was pregnant. I didn't know it at the time, but my mother was, too. I still thought that they should all be spending a great deal more time with me. So one day I decided I'd run away, thereby forcing them to worry about me, and then act like parents."

She smiled as if at the memory, but it wasn't a happy smile. And later Dominik would have to reflect on how and why he knew the difference between her *smiles*, God help him. As if he'd made a study against his will, when he wasn't entirely paying attention.

"I rode the buses around and around, well into the evening," she said with that same smile. "And they came together, just as I'd hoped, but only so they could blame each other for what a disaster I was. Within an hour of my return they'd agreed to send me off to boarding school for the summer, so others could deal with me and they wouldn't have to do it themselves."

"I understand that not all parents are good ones," Dominik said, his voice low. "But I would caution you against complaining about your disengaged, yet present, parents while in the presence of a man who had none. Ever. Disengaged or otherwise."

"I'm not complaining about them," Lauren replied quietly. "They are who they are. I'm telling you how I came to be at a very posh school for summer. It was entirely filled with children nobody wanted."

"Pampered children, then. I can assure you no orphanage is *posh*."

"Yes. Someone, somewhere, paid handsomely to send us all to that school. But it would have been hard to tell a lonely nine-year-old, who knew she was at that school because her parents didn't want anything to do with her, that she was *pampered*. Mostly, I'm afraid, I was just scared."

Dominik stared back at her, telling himself he felt nothing. Because he ought to have felt nothing. He had taught her that sensation was real and that she could feel it, but he wanted none of it himself. No sensation. No emotion.

None of this scraping, aching thing that lived in him now that he worried might crack his ribs open from the inside. Any minute now.

"They taught us manners," Lauren told him in the same soft, insistent tone. "Comportment. Dancing. And it all seemed as stupid to me as I'm sure it does to you right now, but I will tell you this. I have spent many an evening since that summer feeling out of place. Unlike everyone else my age at university, for example, with all their romantic intrigue. These days I'm often trotted off to a formal affair where I am expected to both act as an emblem for Combe Industries as well as blend into the background. All at once. And do you know what allows me to do that? The knowledge that no matter what, I can handle myself in any social situation. People agonize over which fork to choose and which plate is theirs while I sit there, listening to conversations I shouldn't be hearing, ready and able to do my job."

"Heaven forbid anything prevent you from doing your job."

"I like my job."

"Do you? Or do you like imagining that your Mr. Combe cannot make it through a day without you?" He shrugged when she glared at him. "We are all of us dark creatures in our hearts, little red. Think of the story from the wolf's point of view next time. Our Red Riding Hood doesn't come off well, does she?"

He thought she had quite a few things to say to that, but she nodded toward the silverware before them instead. "We'll work from the outside in, and as we go we'll work on appropriate dinner conversation at formal occasions, which does not include obsessive references to fairy tales."

Dominik couldn't quite bring himself to tell her that he already knew how to handle a formal dinner, thank you. Not when she thought she was giving him a tool he could use to *save himself*, no less.

Just as he couldn't bring himself—allow himself—to tell her all those messy things that sloshed around inside him at the thought of her as a scared nine-year-old, abandoned by her parents and left to make *manners* her sword and shield.

He showed her instead, pulling her onto his lap before one of the interminable courses and imparting his own lesson. Until they were both breathing too heavily to care that much whether they used the correct fork—especially when his fingers were so talented.

He meant to leave the following day, but there was dancing, which meant he got to hold Lauren in his arms and then sweep her away upstairs to teach her what those bed posts were for. He meant to leave the day after that, but she'd had videos made of all the San Giacomo holdings.

There was something every day. Presentations on all manner of topics. Lessons of every description, from comportment to conversation and back again. Meetings with the unctuous, overly solicitous tailors, who he wanted to hate until they returned with beautiful clothes even he could tell made him look like the aristocrat he wasn't.

Which he should have hated—but couldn't, not when Lauren looked at him as if he was some kind of king.

He needed to get out of there, but he had spent an entire childhood making up stories about his imaginary family in his head. And he didn't have it in him to walk away from the first person he'd ever met who could tell him new stories. Real stories, this time.

Because Lauren also spent a significant part of every day teaching him the history of the San Giacomos, making sure he knew everything there was to know about their rise to power centuries ago. Their wealth and consequence across the ages.

And how it had likely come to pass that a sixteen-year-old heiress had been forced to give up her illegitimate baby, whether she wanted to or not.

He found that part the hardest to get his head around—likely because he so badly wanted to believe it.

"You must have known her," he said one day as summer rain danced against the windows where he stood.

They were back in the library, surrounded

by all those gleaming, gold-spined books that had never been put on their self-important shelves for a man like him, no matter what blood ran in his veins. Lauren sat with her tablet before her, stacks of photo albums arrayed on the table, and binders filled with articles on the San Giacomo family. All of them stories that were now his, she told him time and time again. And all those stories about a family that was now his, too.

Dominik couldn't quite believe in any of it.

He'd spent his childhood thirsty for even a hint of a real story to tell about his family. About himself. Then he'd spent his adulthood resolved not to care about any of it, because he was making his own damned story.

He couldn't help thinking that this was all…too late. That the very thing that might have saved him as a child was little more than a bedtime story to him now, with about as much impact on his life.

"Alexandrina," he elaborated when Lauren frowned at him. "You must have known my mother while she was still alive."

And he didn't know how to tell her how strange those words felt in his mouth. *My mother.* Bitter and sweet. Awkward. Unreal. *My mother* was a dream he'd tortured himself with as a boy. Not a real person. Not a real woman with a life, hopes and dreams and possibly even *reasons.*

It had never occurred to him that his anger was a gift. Take that away and he had nothing but the urge to find compassion in him somewhere…and how was a man meant to build his life on that?

"I did know her," Lauren said. "A little."

"Was she…?"

But he didn't know what to ask. And he wasn't sure he wanted to know the answers.

"I couldn't possibly be a good judge." Lauren was choosing her words carefully. And Dominik didn't know when he'd become so delicate that she might imagine he needed special handling. "I worked for her son, so we were never more than distantly polite the few times we met. I don't know that any impression I gleaned of her would be the least bit worthwhile."

"It is better than no impressions, which is what I have."

Lauren nodded at that. "She was very beautiful."

"That tells me very little about her character, as I think you know."

"She could be impatient. She could be funny." Lauren thought a moment. "I think she was very conscious of her position."

"Meaning she was a terrible snob."

"No, I don't think so. Not the way you mean it. I never saw her treat anyone badly. But she had certain standards that she expected to have met." She smiled. "If she was a man, people would say she knew her own mind, that's all."

"I've read about her." And he had, though he had found it impossible to see anything of him in the impossibly glamorous creature who'd laughed and pouted for the cameras, and inspired so many articles about her *style*, which Dominik suspected was a way to talk about a high-class woman's looks without causing offense. "She seemed entirely defined by her love affairs and scandals."

"My abiding impression of her was that she had learned how to be pretty. And how to use that prettiness to live up to the promise of both the grand families she was a part of. But I don't think it ever occurred to her that she could be happy."

"Could she?" Dominik asked, sardonic straight through. "I didn't realize that was on offer."

"It should always be on offer," Lauren replied with a certain quiet conviction that Dominik refused to admit got to him. Because it shouldn't have. "Isn't that the point?"

"The point of what, exactly?"

"Everything, Dominik."

"You sound like an American advertisement," Dominik said after a moment, from between his teeth. "No one is owed happiness. And certainly, precious few find it."

He hadn't meant to move from the windows, but he had. And he was suddenly standing in front of that sofa, looking down at Lauren.

Who gazed straight back at him, that same softness on her face. It connected directly to that knot inside him he'd been carrying for weeks now. That ache. That infernal clamoring on the inside of his ribs that demanded he leave, yet wouldn't let him go.

"Maybe if we anticipated happiness we might find a little along the way." Her voice was like honey, and he knew it boded ill. He knew it was bad for him. Because he had no defenses against that kind of sweetness. Caramel eyes and honey voice—and he was a goner. "Why not try?"

"I had no idea that our shabby little marriage of convenience would turn so swiftly into an encounter group," he heard himself growl. When she didn't blanch at that the way he'd expected she would, he pushed on. "So-called happiness is the last refuge and resort of the dim-witted. And those who don't know any better, which I suppose is redundant. I think you'll find the real world is a little too complicated for platitudes and whistling as you work."

Lauren lifted one shoulder, then dropped it. "I don't believe that."

And it was the way she said it that seemed to punch holes straight through Dominik's chest. There was no defiant tilt to her chin. There was no angry flash of temper in her lovely eyes. It was a simple statement, more powerful somehow for its softness than for any attempt at a show of strength.

And there was no reason he should feel it shake in him like a storm.

"You don't believe that the world is a terrible place, as complicated as it is harsh, desperate people careening about from greed to self-interest and back again? Ignoring their children or abandoning them in orphanages as they see fit?"

"The fact that people can be awful and scared only means that when we happen upon it, we should cling to what happiness we can."

"Let me guess. You think I should be more grateful that after all this time, the woman who clearly knew where I was all along told others where to find me. But only after her death, so they could tell me sad stories about how she *might* have given me away against her will. You want me to conclude that I ended up here all the same, so why dwell on what was lost in the interim? You will have to forgive me if I do not see all this as the gift you do."

"The world won't end if you allow the faintest little gleam of optimism into your life," Lauren said with that same soft conviction that got to him in ways he couldn't explain. And didn't particularly want to analyze. "And who knows? You could even allow yourself to hope for something. Anything. It's not dim-witted and it's not because a person doesn't see the world as it is." Her gaze was locked to his. "Hope takes strength, Dominik. Happiness takes work. And I choose to believe it's worth it."

"What do you know of either?" he demanded. "You, who locked yourself away from the world and convinced yourself you disliked basic human needs. You are the poster child for happiness?"

"I know because of you."

The words were so simple.

And they might as well have been a tornado, tearing him up.

"Me." He shook his head as if he didn't understand the word. As if she'd used it to bludgeon him. "If I bring you *happiness*, little red, I fear you've gone and lost yourself in a deep, dark woods from which you will never return."

She stood up then, and he was seized with the need to stop her somehow. As if he knew what she was going to say when of course, he couldn't know. He refused to know.

He should have left before this happened. *He should have left.*

His gaze moved over her, and it struck him that while he'd certainly paid close attention to her, he hadn't truly *looked* at her since they'd arrived here weeks ago. Not while she was dressed. She wasn't wearing the same sharp, pointedly professional clothing any longer—and he couldn't recall the last time she had. Today she wore a pair of trousers he knew were soft like butter, and as sweetly easy to remove. She wore a flowing sort of top that drooped down over one shoulder, which he liked primarily because it gave him access to the lushness beneath.

Both of those things were clues, but he ignored them.

It was the hair that was impossible to pretend hadn't changed.

Gone was the sleek ponytail, all that blond silk ruthlessly tamed and controlled. She wore it loose now, tumbling around her shoulders, because he liked his hands in it.

Had he not been paying attention? Or had he not wanted to see?

"Yes, you," she said, answering the question he'd asked, and all the ones he hadn't. "You make me happy, Dominik. And hopeful. I'm sorry if that's not what you want to hear."

She kept her gaze trained on his, and he didn't know what astounded him more. That she kept saying these terrible, impossible things. Or that she looked so fearless as she did it, despite the color in her cheeks.

He wanted to tell her to stop, but he couldn't seem to move.

And she kept right on going. "I thought I knew myself, but I didn't. I thought I knew what I needed, but I had no idea. I asked you to teach me and I meant very specifically about sex. And you did that, but you taught me so much more. You taught me everything." She smiled then, a smile he'd never seen before, so tremulous and full of hope—and it actually hurt him. "I think you made me whole, Dominik, and I had no idea I wasn't already."

If she had thrust a sword into the center of his chest, then slammed it home, he could not have felt more betrayed.

"I did none of those things," he managed to grit out. "Sex is not happiness. It is not hope. And it is certainly no way to go looking for yourself, Lauren."

"And yet that's who I found." And she was still aiming that smile at him, clearly unaware that she was killing him. "Follow the bread crumbs long enough, even into a terrible forest teeming with scary creatures and wolves like men, and there's no telling what you'll find at the other end."

"I know exactly what you'll find on the other end. Nothing. Because there's no witch in a gingerbread house. There's no Big Bad Wolf. You were sent to find me by a man who was executing a duty, nothing more. And I came along with you because—"

"Because why, exactly?" Again, it was the very softness and certainty in her voice that hit him like a gut punch. "You certainly didn't have to invite me into your cabin. But you did."

"Something I will be questioning for some time to come, I imagine." Dominik slashed a hand through the air, but he didn't know if it was aimed at her—or him. "But this is over, Lauren. You had your experiment and now it's done."

"Because I like it too much?" She had the audacity to laugh. "Surely, you've done this before, Dominik. Surely, you knew the risks. If you open someone up, chances are, they're going to like it. Isn't that what you wanted? Me to fall head over heels in love with you like every virgin cliché ever? Why else would you have dedicated yourself to *my experiment* the way you did?"

He actually backed away from her then. As if the word she'd used was poison. Worse than that. A toxic bomb that could block out the sun.

It felt as if she'd blinded him already.

"There is no risk whatsoever of anyone falling in love with me," he told her harshly.

"I think you know that isn't true." She studied him as if he'd disappointed her, as if he was *currently* letting her down, right there in full view of all the smug volumes of fancy books he'd never read and never would. "I assumed that was why you stayed all this time."

"I stayed all this time because that was the deal we made."

"The deal we made was for a wedding

night, Dominik. Maybe a day or so after. It's been nearly two months."

"It doesn't matter how long it's been. It doesn't matter why. I'm glad that you decided you can feel all these emotions." But he wasn't glad. He was something far, far away from *glad*. "But I don't. I won't."

"But you do." And that was the worst yet. Another betrayal, another weapon. Because it was so matter-of-fact. Because she stared right back at him as if she knew things about him he didn't, and that was unbearable. Dominik had never been *known*. He wanted nothing to do with it. "I think you do."

And Dominik never knew what he might have said to that—how he might have raged or, more terrifying, how he might not have— because the doors to the library were pushed open then, and one of Combe Manor's quietly competent staff members stood there, frowning.

"I'm sorry to interrupt," she said, looking back and forth between them. "But something's happened, I'm afraid." She gestured in the direction of the long drive out front. "There are reporters. Everywhere. Cameras, microphones and shouting."

The maid's eyes moved to Dominik, and he thought she looked apologetic. When all he could feel was that emptiness inside him that had always been there and always would. Even if now, thanks to Lauren, it ached.

The maid cleared her throat. "They're calling for you, sir. By name."

CHAPTER TWELVE

IN THE END, Lauren was forced to call the Yorkshire Police to encourage the paparazzi to move off the property, down to the bottom of the long drive that led to Combe Manor from the village proper and away from the front of the house itself.

But the damage was done. The will had been leaked, as Lauren had known it would be eventually, and Dominik had been identified. That he had quietly married his half brother's longtime personal assistant had made the twenty-four-hour news cycle.

She quickly discovered that she was nothing but a shameless gold digger. There was arch speculation that Matteo had dispatched her to corral Dominik, marry him under false pretenses and then…work him to Matteo's advantage somehow.

It was both close to the truth and nothing like the truth at all, but any impulse she might have had to laugh at it dissipated in the face of Dominik's response.

Which was to disappear.

First, he disappeared without actually going anywhere. It was like looking into a void. One moment she'd been having a conversation—admittedly, not the most pleasant conversation—with him. The next, it was as if the Dominik she'd come to know was gone and a stranger had taken his place.

A dark, brooding stranger, who looked at her with icy disinterest. And as far as she could tell, viewed the paparazzi outside the same. He didn't call her *little red* again, and she would have said she didn't even like the nickname.

But she liked it even less when he stopped using it.

Her mobile rang and rang, but she ignored the calls. From unknown numbers she assumed meant more reporters. From Pia, who had likely discovered that she had another brother from the news, which made Lauren feel guilty for not insisting Matteo tell her earlier. And from the various members of the Combe Industries Board of Directors, which she was more than happy to send straight to voice mail.

"It's Mr. Combe," she said when it rang another time. "At last."

"You must take that, of course," Dominik said, standing at the windows again, glaring off into the distance. "Heaven forfend you do not leap to attention the moment your master summons you."

And Lauren couldn't say she liked the way he said that. But she didn't know what to do about it, either.

"We always knew this day would come," she told him, briskly, when she'd finished having a quick damage control conversation with Matteo. "It's actually surprising that didn't happen sooner."

"We have been gilding this lily for weeks now," Dominik replied, his voice that dark growl that made everything in her shiver— and not entirely from delight. "We have played every possible Pygmalion game there is. There is nothing more to be accomplished here."

"Where would you like to go instead?" She had opened up the cabinet and turned on the television earlier, so they could watch the breathless news reports and the endless scroll of accusation and speculation at the bottom of the screen. Now she turned the volume up again so she could hear what they were saying. About her. "I suppose we should plan some kind of function to introduce you to—"

":No."

"No? No, you don't want to be introduced to society? Or no, you don't want—"

"You fulfilled your role perfectly, Lauren." But the way he said it was no compliment. It was…dangerous. "Your Mr. Combe will be so proud, I am sure. You have acted as my jailer. My babysitter. And you have kept me out of public view for very nearly two months, which must be longer than any of you thought possible. You have my congratulations. I very nearly forgot your purpose in this."

His voice didn't change when he said that. And he didn't actually reach out and strike her.

But it felt as if he did.

"I thought this would happen sooner, as a matter of fact," Lauren managed to say, her heart beating much too wildly in her chest. Her head spinning a little from the hit that hadn't happened. "And my brief was to give you a little polish and a whole lot of history, Dominik. That's all. I found a hermit in a hut. All Mr. Combe asked me to do was make you a San Giacomo."

"And now I am as useless as any one of

them. You've done your job well. You are clearly worth every penny he pays you."

It was harder to keep her cool than it should have been. Because she knew too much now. He was acting like a stranger, but her body still wanted him the way it always did. He had woken her this morning by surging deep inside her, catapulting her from dreams tinged with the things he did to her straight into the delirious reality.

She didn't know how to handle this. The distance between them. The fury in his dark gaze. The harsh undercurrent to everything he said, and the way he looked at her as if she had been the enemy all along.

She should have known that the price of tasting happiness—of imagining she could—meant that the lack of it would hurt her.

More than hurt her. Looking at him and seeing a stranger made her feel a whole lot closer to broken.

She should have known better than to let herself *feel*.

"I know this feels like a personal attack," she said, carefully, though she rather thought she'd been the one personally attacked. "But this is about how the San Giacomo and Combe families are perceived. And more, how Matteo and his sister have been portrayed in the press in the wake of their father's death. No one wanted you to be caught up in that."

"And yet here I am."

"Dominik. Please. This is just damage control. That's the only reason Mr. Combe didn't proclaim your existence far and wide the moment he knew of you."

That gaze of his swung to her and held. Hard, like another blow. It made her want to cry—but she knew, somehow, that would only make it worse.

"You cannot control damage, Lauren. I would think you, of all people, would know this. You can only do your best to survive it."

And she had no time to recover from that.

Because that was when the self-satisfied newscaster on the television screen started talking about who Dominik James really was.

"We've just been made aware that Dominik James is not merely the long-lost heir to two of Europe's most prominent families," the man said. "Our sources tell us he is also a self-made billionaire who ran his own security company until he sold it recently for what is believed to be a small fortune in its own right. Dominik himself has been widely sought after by celebrities and kings alike, and a number of governments besides."

Then they flashed pictures of him, in case Lauren had somehow missed the implications. There were shots of Dominik in three-piece suits, his hair cropped close to his head, shaking hands with powerful, recognizable men. In and out of formal balls, charity events and boardrooms.

Nothing like a feral hermit at all.

"Oh, dear," Dominik said when the newscast cut to some inane commercial, too much darkness in his voice. "Your table settings will not save you now, Lauren. It has all been a lie. I am not at all who you thought I was. Why don't you tell me more about how happy you are?"

And Lauren remembered exactly why she'd decided emotion wasn't for her. She had been nine years old and sent off to a terrifying stone building filled with strangers. She'd stayed awake the whole of that first night, sobbing into her pillow so her roommate didn't hear her.

Since then, she'd forgotten that these terrible emotions could sit on a person like this. Crushing her with their weight. Suffocating her, yet never quite killing her.

Making her own heartbeat feel like an attack.

"You didn't need me at all," she managed

to say, parts of her breaking apart on the inside like so many earthquakes, stitched together into a single catastrophe she wasn't sure she would survive. No matter what he'd said about damage.

But she didn't want to let him see it.

"No," Dominik said, and there was something terrible there in his gray eyes that made her want to reach out to him. Soothe him somehow. But his voice was so cold. Something like cruel, and she didn't dare. "I never needed you."

"This was a game, then." She didn't know how she was speaking when she couldn't feel her own face. Her outsides had gone numb, but that paralysis did not extend inside, where she was desperately trying to figure out what to do with all that raw upheaval before it broke her into actual pieces. "You were just playing a game. I can understand that you wanted to find out who your family really was. But you were playing the game with me."

And maybe later she would think about how he stood there, so straight and tall and bruised somehow, that it made her ache. With that look on his face that made her want to cry.

But all she could do at the moment was

fight to stay on her feet, without showing him how much he was hurting her. It was crucial that she swallow that down, hide it away, even as it threatened to cut her down.

"Life is damage, Lauren," he said in that same dark, cold way. "Not hope. Not happiness. Those are stories fools tell to trick themselves into imagining otherwise. The true opiate of the masses. The reality is that people lie. They deceive you. They abandon you whenever possible, and may use you to serve their own ends. I never needed you to polish me. But you're welcome all the same. Someday you'll thank me for disabusing you of all these damaging notions."

Her mobile rang again, Matteo's name flashing on her screen.

And for the first time in as long as she could remember, Lauren didn't want to answer. She wanted to fling her mobile across the room and watch it shatter against the wall. Part of her wanted very much to throw it at Dominik, and see if it would shatter that wall.

But she did neither.

She looked down at the mobile, let her thoughts turn violent, and when she looked up again Dominik was gone.

And she sat where she was for a very long time, there on a Combe family sofa before a television screen that repeated lie after lie about who she was until she was tempted to believe it herself.

Her mobile rang. It rang and rang, and she let it.

Outside, the endless summer day edged into night, and still Lauren sat where she was.

She felt hollowed out. And yet swollen somehow. As if all those unwieldy, overwhelming emotions she'd successfully locked away since she was a child had swept back into her, all at once, until she thought they might break her wide open.

It was the first time in almost as long that she didn't have the slightest idea what to do. How to fix this. Or even if she wanted to.

All she knew was that even now, even though Dominik had looked at her the way he had, and said those things to her, he was still the one she wanted to go to. It was his arms she longed for. His heat, his strength.

How could she want him to comfort her when he was the one who had hurt her?

But she wasn't going to get an answer to that question.

Because when she went looking for him, determined to figure at least some part of this out, she discovered that Dominik hadn't simply disappeared while he'd stood there before her.

He'd actually gone.

He'd packed up his things, clearly, as there was nothing to suggest he'd been here at all. And then he must have let himself out while she'd been sitting there in the library where he'd left her, trying her best not to fall apart.

And she didn't have to chase after him to know he had no intention of coming back.

Because she had fallen for him, head over heels. But he had only ever been playing a game.

And Lauren would have to learn to live with that, too.

Lauren launched herself back into her life.

Her real life, which did not include mysterious men with hidden fortunes who lived off in the Hungarian woods. The life she had built all by herself, with no support from anyone.

The life that she was sure she remembered loving, or at least finding only a few months ago.

"You still love it," she snapped at herself one morning, bustling around her flat on her way to work. "You love every last part of it."

"You know when you start talking to yourself," Mary said serenely, splashing the last of the milk into her tea, "that's when the stress has really won."

Lauren eyed her roommate and the empty jug of milk. "Is that your mobile ringing?"

And as Mary hurried out of the room, she told herself that she was fine. Good.

Happy and hopeful, as a matter of fact, because neither one of those things had anything to do with the surly, angry man who'd done exactly what she'd asked him to do and then left after staying much longer than she'd expected he would.

She had what she wanted. She knew what other people felt. She understood why they went to such great lengths to have sex whenever possible. And she was now free to go out on the pull whenever she pleased. She could do as Dominik had once suggested and take herself off to a local pub, where she could continue conducting the glorious experiment in her own sexual awakening. On her own.

He didn't need her. And she certainly didn't need him.

Lauren decided she'd get stuck into it, no pun intended, that very night.

She thought about it all day long. She made her usual assenting, supportive sounds during the video conference from wherever Matteo was in the world today, but what she was really thinking about was the debauchery that awaited her. Because Dominik had been no more than a means to an end, she told herself. Merely a stepping-stone to a glorious sensual feast.

She left work early—which was to say, on time for once—and charged into the first pub she saw.

Where she remained for the five minutes it took to look around, see all the men who weren't Dominik and want to cry.

Because it turned out that the only kind of awakening she wanted was with him.

Only and ever with him, something in her said with a kind of finality that she felt knit itself inside her like bone.

And maybe that was why, some six weeks after the tabloids had discovered Dominik—when all that bone had grown and gotten strong—she reacted to what ought to have been a perfectly simple request from Matteo the way she did.

"I'll be landing in San Francisco shortly," he told her from his jet.

"And then headed home, presumably," she interjected. "To attend to your empire."

"Yes, yes," he said in a way that she knew

meant, *or perhaps not*. "But what I need you to do is work on that marriage."

Lauren had him on the computer monitor at her desk so she could work more easily on her laptop as he fired his usual instructions at her.

But she stopped what she was doing at that and swiveled in her chair, so she could gaze at him directly.

"Which marriage would that be?" she asked. Tartly, she could admit. "Your sister's? You must know that she and her prince are playing a very specific cat and mouse game—"

Matteo was rifling through papers, frowning at something off screen, and she knew that his sister's romantic life was a sore point for him. Was that why she'd brought it up? When she knew that wasn't the marriage he meant?

"I mean your marriage, Lauren," he said in that distracted way of his. She knew what that meant, too. That her boss had other, more important things on his mind. Something she had always accepted as his assistant, because that was her job—to fade into his background and make certain he could focus on anything he wished. But he was talking about *her*. And the marriage he'd suggested, and she'd actually gone ahead and done on his command. "There's a gala in Rome next week. Do you think your husband is sufficiently tamed? Can he handle a public appearance?"

"Well, he's not actually a trained bear," she found herself replying with more snap in her voice than necessary. "And he was handling public appearances just fine before he condescended to come to Combe Manor. So no need to fear he might snap his chain and devour the guests, I think."

"You can field the inevitable questions from paparazzi," Matteo said, frowning down at the phone in his hand. The way he often did—so there was no reason for it to prick at Lauren the way it did. *Maybe it is time you ask yourself what you* wouldn't *do if your Mr. Combe asked it*, Dominik had said. *You may find the answers illuminating.* But what about what Matteo wouldn't do for her? Like pay attention to the fact she was an actual person, not a bit of machinery? "You know the drill."

"Indeed I do. I know all the drills."

She'd created the drills, for that matter. And she wasn't sure why she wanted to remind Matteo of that.

"Just make sure it looks good," Matteo said, and he looked at her then. "You know what I mean. I want a quiet, calm appearance that makes it clear to all that the San Giacomo scandal is fully handled. I want to keep the board happy."

"And whether the brother you have yet to meet is happy with all these revelations about the family he never knew is of secondary interest, of course. Or perhaps of no interest at all."

She was sure she'd meant to say that. But there it was, out there between them as surely as if she'd hauled off and slapped her boss in the face.

Matteo blinked, and it seemed to Lauren as if it took a thousand years for him to focus on her.

"Is my brother unhappy?" he asked. Eventually.

"You will have to ask him yourself," she replied. And then, because she couldn't seem to stop herself, "He's your brother, not mine."

"He is your husband, Lauren."

"Do you think it is the role of a wife to report on her husband to her boss? One begins to understand why you remain unmarried."

Something flashed over his face then, and she didn't understand why she wasn't already apologizing. Why she wasn't hurrying to set things right.

"You knew the role when you took it." Matteo frowned. "Forgive me, but am I missing something?"

And just like that, something in Lauren snapped.

"I am your personal assistant, Mr. Combe," she shot at him. "That can and has included such things as sorting out your wardrobe. Making your travel arrangements. Involving myself more than I'd like in your personal life. But it should never have included you asking me to marry someone on your behalf."

"If you had objections you should have raised them before you went ahead and married him, then. It's a bit late now, don't you think?"

"When have I ever been permitted to have objections in this job?" She shook her head, that cold look on Dominik's face flashing through her head. And the way he'd said *your master.* "When have I ever said no to you?"

Matteo's frown deepened, but not because he was having any kind of emotional response. She knew that. She could see that he was baffled.

"I value you, Lauren, if that's what this is about. You know that."

But Lauren wasn't the same person she had been. It wasn't the value Matteo assigned to her ability to do her job that mattered to her. Not anymore.

She could look back and see how all of this had happened. How she, who had never been wanted by anyone, threw herself into being needed instead. She'd known she was doing it. She'd given it her all. And she'd been hired by Matteo straight out of university, so it had felt like some kind of cure of all the things that ailed her to make sure she not only met his needs, but anticipated them, too.

She had thought they were a team. They had been, all these years. While he'd had to work around his father and now he was in charge.

But Dominik had taught her something vastly different than how to make herself indispensable to the person who paid her.

He had taught her how to value herself.

He'd taught her how to want. How to *be wanted*.

And in return, he'd taught her how to want *more*.

Because that was the trouble with allowing herself to want anything at all when she'd done without for so long. She wasn't satisfied with half measures, or a life spent giving everything she had to a man who not only couldn't return it, but whom she didn't want anything from.

She didn't want to sacrifice herself. It turned out that despite her choice of profession, she wasn't a martyr. Or she didn't want to be one.

Not anymore.

She knew what she wanted. Because she knew what it felt like now to be wanted desperately in return—no matter that Dominik might not have admitted that. She still knew.

He had stayed so long at Combe Manor. He had showed her things that she'd never dared dream about before. And he had taken her, over and over again, like a man possessed.

Like a man who feared losing her the same way she'd feared losing him.

If he hadn't cared, he wouldn't have snuck away. She knew that, too.

Lauren looked around the office that was more her home than her flat had ever been. The couch where she'd slept so many nights—including the night before her wedding. The windows that looked out over the city she'd loved so desperately not because she required its concrete and buildings, she understood now, but because it had been her constant. The one kind of parent that wouldn't turn its back on her.

But she didn't need any of these things any longer.

Lauren already had everything she needed. Maybe she always had, but she knew it now. And it was time instead to focus on what she *wanted*.

"And I have valued these years, Mr. Combe," she said now, lifting her head and looking Matteo in the eye. "More than you know. But it's time for me to move on." She smiled when he started to protest. "Please consider this my notice. I will train my replacement. I'll find her myself and make certain she is up to your standards. Never fear."

"Lauren." His voice was kind then.

But it wasn't his kindness she wanted.

"I'm sorry," she said quietly. "But I can't do this anymore."

And that night she lay in her bed in the flat she paid for but hardly knew. She stared at her ceiling, and when that grew old, she moved to look out the window instead.

There was concrete everywhere. London rooftops, telephone wires and the sound of traffic in the distance. The home she'd made. The parent she'd needed. London had been all things to her, but in the end, it was only a city. Her favorite city, true. But if it was any more than that, she'd made it that way.

And she didn't want that any longer. She didn't need it. She craved…something else. Something different.

Something wild, a voice in her whispered.

Lauren thought about want. About need. About the crucial distinction between the two, and why it had taken her so long to see it.

And the next morning she set off for Hungary again.

By the time she made it to the mountain village nestled there at the edge of the forest it was well into the afternoon.

But she didn't let that stop her. She left the hired car near the inn she'd stayed in on the last night of her life before she'd met Dominik and everything changed, and she began to walk.

She didn't mind the growing dark, down there on the forest floor. The temperature dropped as she walked, but she had her red wrap and she pulled it closer around her.

The path was just as she remembered it, clear and easy to follow, if hard going against the high, delicate heels she wore. Because of course she wore them.

Lauren might have felt like a new woman. But that didn't mean she intended to betray herself with sensible shoes.

On she walked.

And she thought about fairy tales. About girls who found their way into forests and thought they were lost, but found their way out no matter what rose up to stop them. Especially if what tried to stop them was themselves.

It was only a deep, dark forest if she didn't know where she was going, she told herself. But she did. And all around her were pretty trees, fresh air and a path to walk upon.

No bread crumbs. No sharp teeth and wolves. No witches masquerading as friends, tucked up in enchanted cottages with monstrous roses and questionable pies.

No foreboding, no wicked spells.

There was only Lauren.

And she knew exactly what she wanted.

When she reached the clearing this time, she marched straight through it. There was no one lurking in the shadows on the front porch, but she hadn't really expected there would be. She walked up, anyway, went straight to the front door and let herself in.

The cabin was just as she remembered it. Shockingly cozy and inviting, and entirely too nice. It was a clue, had she bothered to pay attention to it, that the man she'd come to find—her husband—wasn't the mountain man she'd expected he would be.

Best of all, that same man sat before the fire now, watching her with eyes like rain.

"Turn around, Lauren," he said, his voice like gravel. "If you leave now, you'll make it back to the village before full dark. I wouldn't want to be wandering around the woods at night. Not in those shoes. You have no idea what you might encounter."

"I know exactly what I'll find in these woods," she replied. And she let her gaze go where it liked, from that too-long inky-black hair he'd never gotten around to cutting to her specifications to that stern mouth of his she'd felt on every inch of her body. "And look. There you are."

He shook his head. "You shouldn't have come here."

"And yet I did. Without your permission. Much as you ran off from Combe Manor without so much as a hastily penned note."

"I'm sure whatever mission you're on now is just as important as the last one that brought you here to storm about in my forest," he said, and something like temper flashed over his face—though it was darker. Much, much darker. "But I don't care what your Mr. Combe—"

"He didn't send me. I don't work for him anymore, as a matter of fact." She held his gaze and let the storm in it wash over her, too. "This is between you and me, Dominik."

The air between them shifted. Tightened, somehow.

"There is no you and me."

"You may have married me as a joke," she said softly, "but you did marry me. That makes me your wife."

"I need a wife about as much as I need a brother. I don't do family, Lauren. Or jokes. I want nothing to do with any of it."

"That is a shame." She crossed her arms over her chest and she stared him down as if he didn't intimidate her at all. "But I didn't ask you if you needed a wife. I reminded you that you already have one."

"You're wasting your time."

She smiled at him, and enjoyed it when he blinked at that as if it was a weapon she'd had tucked away in her arsenal all this time.

God, she hoped it was a weapon. Because she needed all of those she could find.

And she had no qualms about using each and every one she put her hands on.

"Here's the thing, Dominik," she said, and she wanted to touch him. She wanted to bury her face in the crook of his neck. She wanted to wake up with him tangled all around her. She wanted him, however she could get him. She wanted whatever a life with him looked like. "You taught me how to want. And don't you see? What I want is you."

CHAPTER THIRTEEN

"YOU CAN'T HAVE ME," Dominik growled at her, because that was what he'd decided. It was what made sense. "I never was a toy for you to pick up and put down at will, Lauren. I assumed that was finally clear."

And yet all he wanted to do was get his hands on her.

He knew he couldn't allow that. Even if he was having trouble remembering the *why* of that at the moment, now that she was here. Right here, in front of him, where he'd imagined her no less than a thousand times a night since he'd left England.

But he didn't. Because touching her—losing himself in all that pink and gold sweetness of hers—was where all of this had gone wrong from the start.

"I introduced you to sex, that's all," he said through gritted teeth, because he didn't want to think about that introduction. The way she'd yielded completely, innocent and eager and so hot he could still feel it. As if he carried her inside him. "This is the way of things. You think it means more than it does. But I don't."

"I tested that theory," she told him, and it landed on him like a punch, directly into his gut. "You told me I could walk into any pub in England and have whatever sex I wanted."

"Lauren." And he was surprised he didn't snap a few teeth off, his jaw was so tight. "I would strongly advise you not to stand here in my cabin and brag to me about your sexual exploits."

"Why would you care? If you don't want me?" She smiled at him again, self-possessed and entirely too calm. "But no need to issue warnings or threats. I walked in, took a look around and left. I don't want sexual exploits, Dominik. I told you. I want you."

"No," he growled, despite the way that ache in his chest intensified. "You don't."

"I assure you, I know my own mind."

"Perhaps, but you don't know me."

And he didn't wait for her to take that on board. He surged to his feet, prowling toward her, because she had to understand. She had to understand, and she had to leave, and he had to get on with spending the rest of his life trying to fit the pieces back together.

After she'd torn him up, crumpled him and left him in this mess in the first place.

Because you let her, the voice in him he'd tried to ignore since he'd met her—and certainly since he'd left her—chimed in.

"I thought at first it was the media attention that got to you, but you obviously don't mind that. You've had it before. Why should this be any different?"

And she didn't remind him of his lies of omission. They rose there between them like so much heat and smoke, and still, the only thing he could see was her.

"I don't care about attention." He wanted things he couldn't have. He wanted to *do* something, but when he reached out his hand, all he did was fit it to her soft, warm cheek.

Just to remind himself.

And then he dropped his hand to his side, but that didn't make it better, because she felt even better than he remembered.

"Dominik. I know that you feel—"

"You don't know what I feel." His voice was harsh, but his palm was on fire. As if touching her had branded him, and he was disfigured with it. And maybe it was the fact she couldn't seem to see it that spurred him on. "You don't have great parents, so you think you know, but you don't. There's no doubt that it's your parents who are the problem, not you. You must know this."

"They are limited people," she said, looking taken aback. But she rallied. "I can't deny that I still find it hurtful, but I'm not a little girl anymore. And to be honest, I think they're the ones who are missing out."

"That sounds very adult. Very mature. I commend you. But I'm not you. This is what I'm trying to tell you." And then he said the thing he had always known, since he was a tiny child. The thing he'd never said out loud before. The thing he had never imagined he even needed to put into words, it was so obvious. "There's something wrong with me, Lauren."

Her eyes grew bright. And he saw her hands curl into fists at her sides.

"Oh, Dominik." And he would remember the way she said his name. Long after she was gone, he would replay it again and again, something to warm him when the weather turned cold. It lodged inside him, hot and shining where his heart should have been. "There's nothing wrong with you. Nothing."

"This is not opinion. This is fact." He shook his head, harshly, when she made to reach for him. "I was six days old when I arrived in the orphanage. And brand-new babies never stay long in orphanages, because there are always those who want them. A clean slate. A new start. A child they can pretend they birthed themselves, if they want. But no one wanted me. Ever."

She was still shaking her head, so fiercely it threatened the hair she'd put in that damned ponytail as if it was her mission to poke at him.

"Maybe the nuns are the ones who wanted you, Dominik. Did you ever think of that? Maybe they couldn't bear to give you up."

He laughed at that, though it was a hollow sound, and not only because her words had dislodged old memories he hadn't looked at in years. The smiling face of the nun they'd called Sister Maria Ana, who had treated him kindly when he was little, until cancer stole her away when he was five. How had he forgotten that?

But he didn't want to think about that now. The possibility that someone had been kind to him didn't change the course of his life.

"Nobody wanted me. Ever. With one or two people in your life, even if they are your parents, this could be coincidence. Happenstance. But when I tell you that there is not one person on this earth who has ever truly wanted me, I am not exaggerating." He shoved those strange old memories aside. "There's something wrong with me inside, Lauren. And it doesn't go anywhere. If you can't see it, you will. In time. I see no point in putting us both through that."

Because he knew that if he let her stay, if he let her do this, he would never, ever let her go. He knew it.

"Dominik," she began.

"You showed me binders full of San Giacomos," he growled at her. "Century upon century of people obsessed with themselves and their bloodlines. They cataloged every last San Giacomo ever born. But they threw me away. *She* threw me away."

"She was sixteen," Lauren said fiercely, her red cloak all around her and emotion he didn't want to see wetting her cheeks. But he couldn't look away. "She was a scared girl who did what her overbearing father ordered her to do, by all accounts. I'm not excusing her for not doing something later, when she could have. But you know that whatever else happened, she never forgot you. She knew your name and possibly even where you lived. I can't speak for a dead woman, Dominik, but I think that proves she cared."

"You cannot care for something you throw away like trash," he threw at her.

And her face changed. It…crumpled, and he thought it broke his heart.

"You mean the way you did to me?" she asked.

"I left you before it was made perfectly obvious to you and the rest of the world that I don't belong in a place like that. I'm an orphan. I was a street kid. I joined the army because I wanted to die for a purpose, Lauren. I never meant for it to save me."

"All of that is who you were, perhaps," she said with more of that same ferocity that worked in him like a shudder. "But now you are a San Giacomo. You are a self-made man of no little power in your own right. And you are my husband."

And he didn't understand why he moved closer to her when he wanted to step away. When he wanted—needed—to put distance between them.

Instead, his hands found their way to her upper arms and held her there.

He noticed the way she fit him, in those absurd shoes she wore just as well as when she was barefoot. The way her caramel-colored eyes locked to his, seeing far too much.

"I don't have the slightest idea how to be a husband."

"Whereas my experience with being a wife is so extensive?" she shot right back.

"I don't—"

"Dominik." And she seemed to flow against him until she was there against his chest, her head tipped back so there was nothing else in the whole of the world but this. Her. "You either love me or you don't."

He knew what he should say. If he could spit out the words he could break her heart, and his, and free her from this.

He could go back to his quiet life, here in the forest where no one could disappoint him and he couldn't prove, yet again, how little he was wanted.

Dominik knew exactly what he should say.

But he didn't say it.

Because she was so warm, and he had never understood how cold he was before she'd found him here. She was like light and sunshine, even here in the darkest part of the forest.

And he hadn't gone with her to England because she was an emissary from his past. He certainly hadn't married her because she could tell him things he could have found out on his own about the family that wanted to claim him all of a sudden.

The last time Dominik had done something he didn't want to do, simply because someone else told him to do it, he'd been in the army.

He could tell himself any lie at all, if he liked—and Lord knew he was better at that by the day—but he hadn't married this woman for any reason at all save one.

He'd wanted to.

"What if I do?" he demanded, his fingers gripping her—but whether to hold her close or keep her that crucial few inches away, he didn't know. "What do either one of us know about love, of all things?"

"You don't have to know a thing about love." And she was right there before him, wrapping her arms around his neck as if she belonged there. And fitting into place as if they'd been puzzle pieces, all this time, meant to interlock just like this. "Think about fairy tales. Happy-ever-after is guaranteed by one thing and one thing only."

"Magic?" he supplied. But his hands were moving. He tugged the elastic from her gleaming blond hair and tossed it aside. "Terrible spells, angry witches and monsters beneath the bed?"

"What big worries you have," she murmured, and she was smiling again. And he found he was, too.

"All the better to save you with, little red," he said. "If you'll let me."

"I won't." She brushed his mouth with hers. "Why don't we save each other?"

"I don't know how."

"You do." And when he frowned at her, she held him even closer, until that ache in his chest shifted over to something sweeter. Hotter. And felt a lot like forever. "Happy-ever-after is saving each other, Dominik. All it takes is a kiss."

And this was what she'd been talking about in that sprawling house in Yorkshire.

Hope. The possibility of happiness.

Things he'd never believed in before. But it was different, with her.

Everything was different with her.

So he gathered her in his arms, and he swept her back into the grandest kiss he could give her, right there in their enchanted cottage in the deep, dark woods.

And sure enough, they lived happily ever after.

Just like a fairy tale.

Twelve years later Dominik stood on a balcony that overlooked the Grand Canal in

Venice as night fell on a late summer evening. The San Giacomo villa was quiet behind him, though he knew it was a peace that wouldn't last.

His mouth curved as he imagined the chaos his ten-year-old son could unleash at any moment, wholly unconcerned about the disapproving glares of the ancient San Giacomos who lurked in every dour portrait that graced the walls of this place.

To say nothing of his five-year-old baby girls, a set of the twins that apparently ran in the family, that neither he nor Lauren had anticipated when she'd fallen pregnant the second time.

But now he couldn't imagine living without them. All of them—and well did he remember that he was the man who had planned to live out his days as a hermit, all alone in his forest.

The truth was, he had liked his own company. But he exulted in the family he and Lauren had made together.

The chaos and the glory. The mad rush of family life, mixed in with that enduring fairy tale he hadn't believed in at first—but he'd wanted to. Oh, how he'd wanted to. And so he'd jumped into, feet first, willing to do anything as long as she was with him.

Because she was the only one who had ever wanted him, and she wanted him still.

And he wanted her right back.

Every damned day.

They had built their happy-ever-after, brick by brick and stone by stone, with their own hands.

He had met his sister shortly after Lauren had come and found him in the forest. Pia had burst into that hotel suite in Athens, greeted him as if she'd imagined him into being herself—or had known of him, somehow, in her heart of hearts all this time—until he very nearly believed it himself.

And he'd finally met his brother—in the flesh—sometime after that.

After a perfectly pleasant dinner in one of the Combe family residences—this one in New York City—he and Matteo had stood out on one of the wraparound terraces that offered a sweeping view of all that Manhattan sparkle and shine.

"I don't know how to be a brother," Dominik had told him.

"My sister would tell you that I don't, either," Matteo had replied.

And they'd smiled at each other, and that was when Dominik had started to believe that it might work. This strange new family he would have said he didn't want. But that he had, anyway.

His feelings about Matteo had been complicated, but he'd realized quickly that most of that had to do with the fact Lauren had admired him so much and for so long. Something Matteo put to rest quickly, first by marrying the psychiatrist who had been tasked with his anger management counseling, who also happened to be pregnant with his twin boys. But then he'd redeemed himself entirely in Dominik's eyes by telling Lauren that Combe Industries couldn't function without her.

And then hiring her back, not as his assistant, but as a vice president.

Dominik couldn't have been prouder. And as Lauren grew into her new role in the company she'd given so much of her time and energy, he entertained himself by taking on the duties of the eldest San Giacomo. He found that his brother and sister welcomed the opportunity to allow him to be the face of their ancient family. A role he hadn't realized anyone needed to play, but one it shocked him to realize he was…actually very good at.

He heard the click of very high heels on the marble behind him, and felt his mouth curve.

Moments later his beautiful wife appeared.

᾿e'd taken some or other call in the room set aside in the villa for office purposes, and she was already tugging her hair out of the sleek ponytail she always wore when she had her professional hat on. She smiled back at him as the faint breeze from the water caught her hair, still gleaming gold and bright.

"You look very pleased with yourself," she said. "I can only hope that means you've somehow encouraged the children to sleep. For a thousand hours, give or take."

"That will be my next trick." He shifted so he could pull her into his arms, and both of them let out a small sigh. Because they still fit. Because their puzzle pieces connected even better as time passed. "I was thinking about the banquet last night. And how it was clearly my confident use of the correct spoon midway through that won the assembled patrons of the arts over to my side."

Lauren laughed at that and shook her head at him. "I think what you meant to say was thank you. And you're very welcome. No one knows how difficult it was to civilize you."

He kissed her then, because every kiss was another pretty end with the happy-ever-after that went with it. And better yet, another beginning, stretching new, sweeter stories out before them.

And he wanted nothing more than to lift her into his arms and carry her off to the bed they shared here—another four-poster affair that he deeply enjoyed indulging himself in—but he couldn't. Not yet, anyway.

Because it wasn't only the two of them anymore. And he knew his daughters liked it best when their mama read them stories before bed.

He held her hand in his as they walked through the halls of this ancient place, amazed to realize that he felt as if he belonged here. And he imagined what it might have been like to be raised like this. With two parents who loved him and cared for him and set aside whatever it was they might have been doing to do something like read him a bedtime story.

He couldn't imagine himself in that kind of family. But he'd imagined it for his own kids, and then created it, and he had to think that was better. It was the future.

It was his belief made real, every time his children smiled.

"I love you," Lauren said softly when they reached the girls' room as if she could read every bittersweet line in his heart.

And he knew she could. She always had.

"I love you, too, little red," he told her.

More than he had back then, he thought. More all the time.

And then he stood in the doorway as she swept into the room where her daughters waited. He watched, aware by now that his heart wouldn't actually burst—it would only feel like it might—as his two perfect little girls settled themselves on either side of their gorgeous mother. One with her thumb stuck deep in her mouth. The other with her mother's beautiful smile.

And when his son came up beside him, a disdainful look on his face because he was ten years old and considered himself quite a man of the world, Dominik tossed an arm over the boy's narrow shoulders.

"I'm going to read you a fairy tale," Lauren told the girls.

"Fairy tales aren't real," their son replied. He shrugged when his sisters protested. "Well, they're not."

Lauren lifted her gaze to meet Dominik's, her caramel-colored eyes dancing.

And every time Dominik thought he'd hit his limit, that he couldn't possibly love her more—that it was a physical and emotional impossibility—she raised the bar.

He felt certain that she would keep right on doing it until the day they both died.

And he thought that was what happy-ever-after was all about, in the end.

Not a single kiss, but all the kisses. Down through the years. One after the next, linking this glorious little life of theirs together. Knitting them into one, over and over and over again.

Hope. Happiness. And the inevitable splashes of darkness in between, because life was life, that made him appreciate the light all the more.

And no light shined brighter than his beautiful wife. His own little red.

The love of his life.

"Of course fairy tales are real," he told his son. And his two wide-eyed little girls. Because he was living proof, wasn't he? "Haven't I told you the story of how your mother and I met?"

He ruffled his son's hair. And he kept his eyes on the best thing that had ever wandered into the deep, dark woods, and then straight into his heart.

"Once upon a time, in a land far, far away, a beautiful blonde in a bright red cloak walked into a forest," he said.

"And it turned out," Lauren chimed in, "that the big bad wolf she'd been expecting wasn't so bad, after all."

And that was how they told their favorite story, trading one line for the next and laughing as they went, for the rest of their lives.

* * * * *

If you enjoyed
Untamed Billionaire's Innocent Bride
by Caitlin Crews,
look out for the other stories in her
The Combe Family Scandals trilogy:
The Italian's Twin Consequences,
available now, and Pia's story,
coming soon!

And why not explore these other
Conveniently Wed! stories!

The Sicilian's Bought Cinderella
by Michelle Smart
Crown Prince's Bought Bride
by Maya Blake
Chosen as the Sheikh's Royal Bride
by Jennie Lucas
Penniless Virgin to Sicilian's Bride
by Melanie Milburne

Available now!